KWARGHTTN

Antiquities

Cousin William

ANTIQUITIES

*

Cynthia Ozick

ALFRED A. KNOPF
NEW YORK
2021

THIS IS A BORZOI BOOK
PUBLISHED BY ALFRED A. KNOPF

www.aaknopf.com

Knopf, Borzoi Books, and the colophon are registered trademarks
of Penguin Random House LLC.

Library of Congress Cataloging-in-Publication Data
Names: Ozick, Cynthia, author.
Title: Antiquities / Cynthia Ozick.
Description: First edition. | New York : Alfred A. Knopf, [2021] |
Identifiers: LCCN 2020025778 (print) | LCCN 2020025779 (ebook) |
ISBN 9780593318829 (hardcover) | ISBN 9780593318836 (ebook)
Classification: LCC PS3565.Z5 A85 2021 (print) |
LCC PS3565.Z5 (ebook) | DDC 813/.54—dc23
LC record available at https://lccn.loc.gov/2020025778
LC ebook record available at https://lccn.loc.gov/2020025779

Frontispiece © UCL, The Petrie Museum of Egyptian Archaeology
Jacket images: (details, clockwise) (beetle) Rashad Aliyev / Getty
Images; (lotus) Elena Kazanskaya / Shutterstock; (stork) A-Digit /
Getty Images; (center, palm) Aratehortua / Shutterstock; (frame)
ZU_09 /Getty Images; (ornaments) rawpixel
Jacket design by Abby Weintraub

Manufactured in the United States of America
First Edition

TO

Melanie Jackson

who makes things happen

Antiquities

My name is Lloyd Wilkinson Petrie, and I write on the 30th of April, 1949, at the behest of the Trustees of the Temple Academy for Boys, an institution that saw its last pupil thirty-four years ago. I must unfortunately report that of the remaining Trustees, only seven (of twenty-five) survive. Though well advanced in age myself, I am the youngest, and the least infirm but for a tremor of the left hand, yet capable enough at my Remington despite long years of dependence on my secretary, Miss Margaret Stimmer (now deceased). In our continuing capacity as Trustees, we meet irregularly, contingent on health, here in my study, with its mullioned windows looking out on our old maples newly in leaf.

I call it my study, and why not? My father too kept a sequestered space by this name; his tone in speaking of it signaled a preference for solitude, much like my own. The others, who also have tenure here in Temple House, are pleased to designate their present apartments by those old classroom plaques: Fourth Form Alpha, Fifth Form Beta, and so forth. In this way the nomenclature of the Academy lives on, its various buildings having been converted for use in perpetuity as living quarters for the Trustees. It is notable that certain enhancing decorative efforts have been introduced to the interior of the structure, such as ornamental crown moldings, as well as the installation of an imposing crystal chandelier in each apartment. I believe my late wife would have approved of elaborate appointments of this kind, but the constant swaying and tinkling of these dangling beads and teardrops, at the lightest footstep or wafting of air, is in truth more annoyance than comfort.

The former staff are of course long gone, but we are well attended by a pair of robust young men and (lately) merely two matrons, one of foreign origin, and the refectory has been updated (as they term it) with a modern kitchen, including a sizable pantry. In addition, it is especially needful to recall that the common toilets and showers exclusively for the pupils' use, a disagreeable relic of the Academy's early years, were torn down some time ago. Only the chapel has been left as it was, unheated.

It was determined by consensus at our penultimate meeting that what we are about to undertake shall not be a history of the Academy. It is true that the existing History, composed in 1915 at the moment of the Academy's demise, contains certain expressions that would not be considered acceptable today. The local public library, which gladly received this heartfelt work at the time, will no longer permit it to stand on open shelves. Each Trustee, however, owns a leather-bound copy, and may for our immediate purpose consult it if needed, most likely to retrieve a forgotten name.

Our agreed intent, then, is to produce an album of remembrance, a collection of small memoirs meant to stand out from the welter of the past—seven chapters of, if I may borrow an old catchphrase, emotion recollected in tranquility. When completed, it is to be placed in the Academy vault at J. P. Morgan & Co., together with the History and other mementos already deposited therein, including the invaluable portrait of Henry James that once adorned the chapel. It has always been a matter of pride for us that the Academy's physical plant was constructed on what had been the property (a goodly acreage) of the Temple family, cousins to Henry James; it was from these reputable Temples that the Academy gleaned its name. Unhappily, as recorded in the History, this circumstance has led to misunderstanding. That we were on occasion taken for a Mormon edifice, though risible, was difficulty enough. Most unfortunate was the too common suspicion that "Temple" signified something unpleasantly synagogical, so that on many a Sunday morning the chapel's windows (those precious panels of stained glass depicting the Jerusalem of Jesus's time) were discovered to have been smashed overnight. The youngest forms were regularly enlisted to sweep up the shards and stones.

How ironic were these ugly events, given that the Academy's spirit was premised on English religious and scholarly principles. Our teachers, vetted for probity and suitable church affiliation, were styled masters. Our pupils wore blazers embroidered with inspirational insignia, and caps to match. Football (on the British model) was hygienically encouraged. French, Latin, attendance at chapel, and horsemanship were all mandatory, and indeed our earliest headmaster was brought over, at a considerable wage, from Liverpool. And all that in the familiar greenery of Westchester County!

Yet I have thus far engaged in this overly

hasty prologue without having spoken of my own lineage. I am, as stated above, a Petrie. We have had among us men distinguished in jurisprudence, and I retain in their original folders a selection of my grandfather's briefs, uncommonly impressive in that old copperplate hand, together with early letterheads, on fine linen paper, of the family firm, founded by his father. My own father in his youth left the firm briefly to pursue other interests, but was persuaded to return, and I have in my possession a sampling of his estimable contractual instruments, as well as a small private notebook crackling with grains of sand trapped in its worn and brittle spine. (Of this, more anon.) I am told that I have myself a certain prowess in the writing of prose, at least in the idiom appropriate to the law. And while these bloodline emblems of civic dedication hold pride of place in my heart, they do not reach the stratum of distinction, let alone of renown, of yet another Petrie.

Here I speak of William Matthew Flinders Petrie, knighted by the Queen, and more broadly known as the illustrious archaeologist Sir Flinders Petrie, who passed away in his home in a turbulent Jerusalem a scant seven years ago, and is partially interred in the Protestant Cemetery on Mount Zion. (I am obliged to say partially: his head he donated to the Royal College of Surgeons in London.) My father, in addition to his nearly lifelong devotion to the law (though that life was too brief), was enamored of ancient times, and of esoteric maps, and also of genealogy, and thereby successfully traced the degrees of our relationship to this extraordinary man. It is difficult, of course, to judge when a cousin of a certain distance becomes rather more of a stranger than a relation, but in my father's view there were reasons for his feelings of closeness.

I have intimated that my father impulsively broke away from the firm, to the shock of his parents, and more particularly the consternation of his young wife. (Among his papers I have found a browning newspaper clipping of this event, distressingly reported as a scandal.) He did in fact disappear in the blazingly hot summer of 1880, having gone in search of Cousin William (not yet Sir Flinders). At that time the press was infatuated with the spectacular excavations in Egypt, particularly the Great Pyramid of Giza, under the supervision of Cousin William, who was then a youthful prodigy of twenty-eight. My young father, newly married and destined for a vice-presidency, informing no one beforehand, had abruptly departed by steamship through Cadiz to Alexandria, after which he endured a miserable journey overland to the site of the excavations. It must be admitted that he did not go with empty pockets (he took with him money aplenty, privately arranging for further sums from a Spanish bank); nor could he be charged with absconding of funds. To a family firm such as ours, he was, after all, the heir.

It is from my discreet and quietly dispirited mother, in a burst of confession in her seventieth year, and seriously ailing, that I know something of the effects of this perfunctory escapade. With no inkling of its cause, my mother was left

bewildered and distraught, and as week after
week passed with no letter of explanation, and
no notion of my father's destination, she believed
herself in some inscrutable way to be the insti-
gator of his flight, finding reason upon reason
for blame. How could this be? Three months
after a glorious winter wedding, all glittering
whiteness without and within, the fresh snow
still silken and unblemished, the nave lined with
overflowing stands of white roses, rows of white
pearls sewn into her dress, the groom glow-
ing with ardor (and the paternal promise of an
instant increase in earnings), how could this be?
The Wilkinsons, indignant and fearful, took her
away to weep alone in her childhood bedroom;
her inchoate cries of guilt, and her unthinkable
pleas for divorce, however confused and pitiful, had become too alarmingly public. They
enrolled her for a time, she told me, in a well-
appointed nursing home, to assure her calm, and
to conceal their embarrassment, until the wayward husband should return. And at length he

did return, "brown as any darkie," as my mother described him, admirably resuming his place in the firm and at her side. Following my birth, and until the last hours of my mother's life, my father's unaccountable absence in the summer of 1880 was never again to be spoken of.

*

May 26, 1949. I have been compelled to leave off after a period of unexpected illness brought on by a sunny but uncharacteristically cold Spring, when it was decided to hold the most recent meeting of the Trustees outdoors, under the maples, on those ancient yet sturdy wooden benches originally situated there by the Temple family some eighty years before. There was to be a final consensual understanding of the nature of each Trustee's memoir: first, that it not exceed in length more than ten pages; second, that it be confined to an explicit happening lingering in memory and mood, and perhaps in influ-

ence, until this day; third, that it concern childhood only, and nothing beyond; fourth, that an
implacably immovable date be set for completion, lest the indolence of some turn into general
abandonment; and fifth, that it reflect accurately
the atmosphere and principles of the Academy
at the time in which the incident to be recounted
had occurred. Ah, what callings-out of the past
beneath those venerable trees!

I have failed to explain that each of the Trustees, by the terms of the Trust, and by design of
the founders, must once himself have been a
pupil of the Academy, and is thereby personally indebted to that past. Hence we all remember the reprehensible common showers. We all
remember the sacking of the headmaster from
Liverpool due to his inadequate accent and the
misleading Cambridge degree that brought us
those inferior vowels. (I sometimes ponder what
poor Mr. Brackett-Lynn must have thought of
our American vowels.) I might append here that
of our seven extant Trustees, five are widow-

ers, for whom marriage and family have compensated for early dolor, and two, having never married, are childless. I am glad to say that I am among the five, and am myself the father of a son. Eschewing the law, he long ago settled in California to pursue a career in, as he puts it, "film entertainment." (I am no philosopher, my leanings are wholly pragmatic, but I now and then contemplate how perverse is the cycle of familial traits, the capriciousness of an earlier generation unfathomably reappearing in a later one.) Despite this, we are by no means estranged, though the sputter of the long-distance telephone lines sometimes inhibits intimate talk.

Our conference in that redolent place under the burgeoning branches was cut short, as it happened, by a sudden heavy rainstorm, which accounts for my ten days in bed, when I took advantage of my temporary (though distressing) invalidism by reviewing the little I have set down thus far. How dismaying to note the wandering digressions, the lack of proportion, too much told here, not enough there, and how different from the logical composition of a legal brief! First the circumstance, then the argument invoking precedent, and finally the conclusion, all concise and in order, unburdened by excessive rumination. And I have not yet so much as approached the subject of my memoir, which I hope before long to touch on: the presence in the Academy of a fourth-form pupil preposterously called Ben-Zion Elefantin, his Christian name (so to speak) a puzzling provocation, his surname a repeated pretext for ridicule by merciless boys.

Of those boys at that distant time (and well afterward), nearly all were in a way unwanted half-orphans. Fathers, like mine, dead too soon, or mothers, like mine, too melancholy to tend to a son at home. And now that I speak again of my father, I must revert to the notebook referred to above, given to me by my mother directly after my father's death, together with certain other objects that I retain to this very day. The occasion was a rare holiday from school, permitted only that I might attend my father's obsequies, which chanced also to coincide with my tenth birthday. "Here are your father's toys," my mother said (satirically, as I later understood), and added that such things were fit only for a boy of my temperament, who, as she claimed, preferred mooning over chess pieces to skipping with other boys in fresh air. With the vague awareness of a child, I knew that long before my birth my father had journeyed alone to some faraway land, my mother being too ill to accompany him, and that he had returned with an exquisite gift to delight her: a gold ring in the shape of a scarab. (I never saw her wear it.) He brought with him, besides, an assemblage of ancient oddities—souvenirs, it may be, that had appealed to him during his travels. These had been neglected, dusty and untouched for years, in a glass-fronted cabinet in a corner of my father's study, until the morning following his funeral, when I was sent back to the Academy, carrying with me a bulky rattling pouch. I keep these curious treasures here, all in a row, on a shelf above my desk, just as they were, with the exception of one. (Of that one I will soon have more to say.)

As for the notebook, I hardly knew what to do with it. I made, I recall, some small attempts at reading it, but except for a cursory mention of buffaloes and elephants, there was nothing to interest a boy just turned ten, and I thrust it, along with the other things, into the pouch. Today, undeniably, and in light of my family's past, these much-faded writings are of overriding interest. The notebook has the dimensions of a playing card, no thicker than the width of my little finger. A crowded pencilled scribble in my father's recognizable hand, though plainly hurried. The opening pages disappointingly dull, consisting merely of a list drawn up in one lengthy column spilling over several sheets. Why my father kept this inventory I cannot tell. (It is troubling to think that perhaps he was intending to make a life of such implements, never to

return to my mother.) Here I will try the reader's patience by transcribing only a small part of
these jottings, viz.:

sledgehammers	sandbags
handpicks	crates
pickaxes	turias
shovels	measuring tapes
hoes	wheelbarrows
ropes	line levels
crowbars	theodolites
sieves	plaster
buckets	tents
baskets	horses
mallets	

and so forth, though of horses he would have
more to observe. What most struck my father on
his arrival amid the dust and debris and the vol-
canic heat and the ceaseless jabber of the fellahin,
all of them naked to the waist, was the stench of
the horses' droppings, melting and sizzling in the

baking sand; incongruous as it might be, he was all at once reminded of those long-ago riding lessons at the Academy (already well established in my father's time) purported to be requisite among a young man's skills. How strange, he thought, that over such a great distance, and in such disparate scenes, the smell should be exactly the same!

In view of his warm admiration for Cousin William, I fear that my father was disheartened by his first encounter with this remarkable young man, so close in age to his own (my father was then approaching his thirty-first birthday). He was not welcomed as he had hoped to be. To begin with, he was taken aback by his cousin's appearance: the skin of the brow already markedly lined, while the hint of a beard was late in its growth. He seemed simultaneously both a youth and a seasoned elder. His authority was innate and absolute. But for my father, most uncanny of all was this: to look into the face of Cousin William was akin to gazing into a mirror. The brilliant blue of the eye was the same, though set off against bronze, and the bold cast of the jaw, with its slight yet telltale prognathic ridge (which I too have inherited), was unmistakably familial. Yet though Cousin William was tall, my father was significantly taller, and when he was unceremoniously conscripted and sent to toil among the dark and puny fellahin, he loomed over them, he records, like a white pillar. He had in his enthusiasm immediately presented his genealogical findings to his cousin, but was abruptly warned that such fooleries were irrelevant to the work at hand. You can stay, Cousin William told him, if you are willing to pick up a spade. And if you are willing to pay for your keep.

Under the weight and strain of the long, groaning measuring chains, and his labors with pickaxe and ropes, my father soon threw off his own shirt and wound it around his head as a shelter from the blasting Levantine sun. He gradually became indistinguishable in complexion from his companions, who churned around him in their dusky swarms; he even learned a few words of their language. He grew used to the daylong sound of the great sieves skittering and shuddering like tireless dice. Hauling their laden baskets, the women and children crawled to and fro as mindlessly as a procession of beetles. The children looked underfed, and the women in their ragged tunics, or whatever they were, seemed to my father hardly women at all. His tent at night was invaded by insects of inconceivable size. In daylight, wherever the ubiquitous sand with its scatterings of wild brush and grasses gave way to more familiar vegetation, the earth itself had a reddish tint. And in those ferociously brilliant sunsets, even the sand turned red.

My father did indeed pay for his keep, and more: two extra horses, the photographic equipment soon to arrive from Germany, and an occasional repast for the youngest children, much frowned on for its disruption of duty. And still my father was joyful in those infrequent intervals when Cousin William was inclined to engage with him, most usually to lament an impending shortfall of means: after all, they were two civilized men in happy possession of the selfsame civilized tongue! There were even times when Cousin William spoke thrillingly of his plans for the decades ahead: he would search in the Holy Land for all those famed yet lost and buried Biblical cities, among them Lachish and Hinnom, and so many storied others. He meant one day, he said, to open the womb of the land that was the mother of true religion.

In late August, when the season of excavation was brought to a close, my father turned to an unused page in his notebook and requested that Cousin William inscribe it. And here it is now, clear under my present gaze: "From Petrie to Petrie, Giza, Egypt, 1880." And my father's comment below: "Proof that we are of the same blood."

With nothing useful to occupy him now, my father hired a boatman to ferry him across the Nile to Cairo, where he purchased some proper clothing and had a proper bath and settled, like any idle pleasure-seeker, in a lavish hotel, where, I presume, he pondered his fate and his future. Here there is nothing introspective, but for a single word, joined by a question mark: "Ethel?" (My mother's name.) What follows is a brief account of sailing down the Nile in a felucca, together with a chattering guide, all very much in the vein of a commonplace travelogue. Indeed, it reads as if copied from a Baedeker. He describes the green of the water, a massive colony of storks dipping their beaks, a glimpse of an occasional water buffalo, and on the opposite bank, as they were nearing the First Cataract at Aswan, a series of boulders on the fringe of what (so the guide informed him) was an island with a history of its own, littered with the vestigial ruins of forgotten worship. The boulders were huge and gray, like the backs of a herd of elephants, and beyond them a palm-studded outgrowth. But it was not for these vast vertebrae that the island was called Elephantine, my father learned; it had, it was said, the shape of a tusk. And here he wrote bluntly in his notebook: "So much for the Nile."

In Cairo he loitered discontentedly, as he admits, too often pestered by street vendors pressing on him what purported to be invaluable relics of this era and that, or original bits of limestone casing salvaged from a nearby pyramid. He passed them by, but not always. He was tempted to believe in material authenticity; Cousin William had inspired him. (At this juncture it behooves me to remark that my father never again came into the presence of Sir Flinders Petrie, though for the remainder of his life he read of Cousin William's archaeological repute with persistent and considerable pride.)

To fill those desolate hours—in the sparseness of his final passages he hardly ever speaks of going home—my father began to frequent the souks with their luring rows of antiquities shops, where he saw and he bought, and sometimes believed, and sometimes did not. The dealers were pleased to educate him. Some objects were precious but likely looted. Others were forgeries, and still others purposeful pretenders from small local factories staffed by assiduous carvers and sculptors; caution was necessary. Let the buyer beware! Still, my father saw and bought, saw and bought, and in one honest shop chose a ring of true gold, in the shape of a scarab, which the merchant assured him, with a wink of his eye, had once belonged not to Queen Nefertiti, but to one of her handmaidens, and even if not, it was anyhow genuine gold. (I must note it again: though this very ring was kept with other such ornaments in a china bowl on her dresser, I never once saw it on my mother's finger.)

And then it was mid-September, and my father came home to my mother, and to his destiny in the family firm.

★

June 17, 1949. The truth is that I am discouraged. I have had to stop and reread and relentlessly subject to sober judgment the narrative above, which because of my father's factual flatness (that meticulous list of tools and devices!) was, to my surprise, less harrowing than I had supposed. My father, as I have already observed, was not given to introspection or disclosure. The motive for his precipitous decamping has never been uncovered, and I believe never will be. My son in Los Angeles, recently learning of this long-hidden chronicle, has asked to inspect it, with the end in mind of transforming its scenes (the Great Pyramid, the Nile, the souks of Cairo, et al.) into some noisome motion picture adventure. He expresses particular interest in my mother's travail, and has gone so far as to suggest a notable actress to embody it. As one would expect, I have categorically refused.

All this contention, thrashed out on the telephone, has left me demoralized. But I am far more apprehensive of what lies ahead: the memoir itself, which I recognize I have not yet adequately adumbrated. Since I have no informing scrawl to rely on, as heretofore, it is as if I must excavate, as in a desert, what lies far below and has no wish to emerge—to wit, my boyhood emotions. And by now I cannot escape telling of my racking affections for Ben-Zion Elefantin. That my friendship with him, unlikely as it was, would taint me, I knew. Willy-nilly, I must in earnest soon begin.

The reader will permit me a word, however, about my colleagues in this venture. If I have been delinquent in my progress herein (out of embarrassment, perhaps, or dread), I am not alone. You will recall that among the preparations for these memoirs, a specific finishing date was strictly agreed on. This somewhat threatening clause was proposed by the pair of fellow Trustees I have characterized as unmarried and childless, hence somewhat childlike themselves. They warned, you will remember, of indolence, intending a charge of procrastination leading to evasion, and of course it came as an accusation crudely directed against my own such tendencies. Yet there is no sign that either one of these gentlemen has written so much as a line. They wake late, apparently giving much attention to their dress. The noticeably younger one is a bit of a dandy, with his colorful vests and his showy silk ties. The two of them dawdle over breakfast in one or the other's apartment (they are wanting in any sense of privacy), and in these long and pleasant summer afternoons sit out under the maples, reading incomprehensible poetry in breathless half-whispers (Gerard Manley Hopkins, I believe, of whom I am satisfied to know nothing). Observing this duo of scrawny elders with their walkers beside them, one our sole nonagenarian, how can I not suppose their theatrics to be but a hollow affectation of youth? And it is certainly indolence. How can I proceed with my own memoir if others take theirs so lightly? Our project, after all, is intended solely to honor the Academy, and merits sincere diligence, humbling though this may be.

As it happens, my own diligence, or my occasional lack of it these warm June days when I am overcome by an unconquerable need to nap, can always be detected. I refer to the tapping of my Remington. Even with my door shut, its clatter can be heard throughout the corridors of Temple House. The others, confined to their silent fountain pens, are not subject to such audible surveillance. I am, as I say, a practical man, and early on took advantage of an opportunity that allowed me to acquire this useful skill. Yet luckily, until her unhappy demise seven years ago, I have never had to do without the competence (and may I add the sweetness?) of Miss Margaret Stimmer. She came to us at the age of eighteen, in response to a notice in the Tribune, and already formidably equipped with a sure command of shorthand. She confessed that she had not yet mastered the typewriter but was ready to learn, and rather winningly flourished before me a manual of instructions purchased that very day. I agreed to take her on provisionally, on the condition that she within three weeks reach a designated speed of performance. Her eagerness was persuasive, and she was winning in other ways: spirited brown eyes, and dangling brown curls, and cheeks charmingly pink—wholly in the absence, I was certain, of any aid of artifice. I observed her slender white fingers, hour after hour, dancing more and more agilely over the keys. Miss Margaret Stimmer served as my secretary for many years, until the death of my dear wife, when she became, and remained, my very good friend.

And it is to her that I owe my own facility at the typewriter. Long after she had grown proficient, she kept in one of the lower drawers of her desk, perhaps as a kind of talisman of her felicitous arrival, the manual of instruction that brought her to us. There were times, when she and all others were gone for the day, and our offices were unpeopled and hushed, in my capacity as partner (my father had seen to my promotion soon after the birth of my son) I would stay behind to review the work of some newly hired young attorney. And often enough what I saw in those regrettable papers would lead me to reflect on the future of the firm: if, say, we were to fall on hard times and were forced to retrench? and if such an eventuality might one day compel me to do without a secretary? A practical man must be resourceful, so that now and then in those quiet nights, at a late and lonely hour, I would—delicately and hesitantly—remove from the lower drawer of Miss Margaret Stimmer's desk that well-worn manual, according to whose guidance I studied and practiced, studied and practiced, repeating difficult combinations again and again. And then I would restore the manual to its drawer, lingering over whatever else might be therein: Miss Margaret Stimmer's fresh daily handkerchiefs, with their particular fragrance, and (somewhat to my disappointment), a compact of rouge, with its little round mirror, and a forgotten pair of lemon-colored chamois gloves. It was pleasant then to picture those nimble white fingers sliding easily into their five clinging tunnels—and once I myself attempted to fit my far thicker and clumsier fingers into Miss Margaret Stimmer's gloves. But it could not be done.

Then let it be noted once more: it is solely because of Miss Margaret Stimmer's fortuitous presence and my consequent expertise at the typewriter, that my colleagues are able to ascertain my progress in the composition of this memoir, while I am entirely in the dark about theirs.

*

June 22, 1949. I have at long last decided to offer a description, as far as I am able, of my father's collection. To my knowledge, it has never been properly appraised, as it ought to have been, by any reputable scholar; but for the purpose of this memoir I scarcely think this remiss. Each piece, or so I speculate, was selected chiefly to gratify my father's interest and adoration, and if the utility of each remained a mystery, so much the better. Many of these pieces, and pieces they are, are instantly identifiable: clay lamps, jugs with handles like ears and spouts like the mouth of a fish, amulets, female figurines, and the like, but many are baffling. All are in a way miniature, either because they are parts broken off from a whole, or were conceived on this small scale. I had carried them to the Academy, as I earlier mentioned, with no notion of where I could keep them. Not on display in my cold little Fifth Form cell, like the foolish feminine bric-a-brac we had at home: this would surely invite jeers. Happily, my writing table had beneath it a small cabinet with wooden doors, with its own lock and key, in which I stored my modest necessities, and I installed them there, still in their pouch—all but one artifact, taller than the others, and untypically intact, only because the bits had been almost seamlessly sealed in place by some master restorer's unknown hand. Its storkish height prevented my concealing it with the others; the height of the shelves was too low. Instead, I deposited it under my bed in a shoebox that had no lid and covered it with a pair of woolen socks.

What am I to call this object? It was a jug like other jugs (I mean a container), but more striking: it was made in the shape of a stork. Its breast was the breast of a stork, high and arched. Its spout was a stork's long tapering bill that flowed from a head with an emerald eye. By emerald I intend not merely the color, but the veritable gem itself, yet only on one side of the head. The other showed an empty socket. The legs were folded at the knee, as if kneeling in water, and it was these knees, showing minute specks of their original red, that formed the object's base. Under the base, when I turned it over, were odd scratchings, grooves worn shallow by some forgotten alphabet.

In the days following my father's burial, or, rather, in the half-dark of the nights when the Academy slept and my door was shut, it became my clandestine habit to pluck this object from its cradle and contemplate its meaning for my father. Why had it attracted him, and why had he brought it from that faraway land? Did he imagine it to be a welcome if exotic ornament for domestic display, certain to please my mother? But I saw that my mother scorned it—she who was otherwise partial to polished decorative vases on this and that decorative little table; and at last my father hid it away. It belonged, she said, to his "mad episode," an episode rarely alluded to and never defined. Or perhaps it was only that she judged it too crude and broken, with its missing eye.

In the dim corridor light that seeped under my door the emerald eye glittered, while the blind eye seemed to vanish away. For a reason I could not say then, and still cannot say now, an uncommon image came to me: I thought of a chalice. But a stork cannot be a chalice. So I called this curious thing by the name its birdlike spirit evoked: I called it a beaker. And because of

the solitary nature of my cell I had little fear of
its discovery.

★

June 23, 1949. It was considered one of the Academy's attractions that each pupil should have his
own room, to be fully in his charge, and also to
compel him to undergo the discipline of cleaning it daily and changing his personal bedsheets
every Saturday morning. (At a later date, when
as Trustee it became my duty to assess expenses,
I saw how these youthful responsibilities conve-
niently lessened the need for house maids.) The
reader will have seen that I speak of my cell. This
term was introduced to us with the arrival of
Mr. Canterbury, the new headmaster recruited
to replace poor Mr. Brackett-Lynn. Mr. Canterbury had pursued divinity studies at Oxford;
his accent was pronounced satisfactory. He was
expected to teach Latin and English Poetry, to
maintain order and propriety, and also to preside

over chapel. His first innovation was to install a carpet over the bare cold floor of his study, and also to secure it with lock and key. His aim above all, he said, was to eliminate certain American vulgarities and to elevate our language in general. When some of the masters, and nearly all of the pupils, objected to "cell" for its aura of incarceration, he insisted that its source was, rather, ecclesial and poetical, and for proof cited Coleridge's "the hall as silent as a cell," whereas, he retorted, our halls rivaled in noise a dungeon of blacksmiths with hammer and tongs. I am glad to say that "cell" did not last, and neither did Mr. Canterbury. His long-serving successor was the Reverend Henry McLeod Greenhill, of Boston, who later assisted in the shutting of the Academy, and whose personal library we still retain following his passing soon afterward.

In this connection, and in one of those anomalies of unexpected confluence, the phrase "hammer and tongs" set down above was repeated a very few hours later, via a most distasteful occurrence. I was accosted at the dinner hour by three of my colleagues, who had formed a committee to denounce me. I was accused of making a racket, of disturbing the peace, of interfering with well-earned sleep, and finally of wielding hammer and tongs (these very words) at unconscionable hours. It is true that on certain days when I have, to my dismay, lost an entire afternoon through napping too long, my conscience has impelled me to take up my memoir somewhat past midnight. (Despite such efforts I remain acutely aware that beyond having uttered the name, I have yet to properly acquaint the reader with my unusual attachment to Ben-Zion Elefantin.)

In fine: I have been upbraided (I mean verbally assaulted) for the nocturnal use of my Remington, which in fact I associate most deeply with remembrance of those long-ago nights in my office. (I may have omitted to mention that the machine I own now is the very one used for many years by Miss Margaret Stimmer.) Yet I can hardly believe it is the sound of my energetic tapping that offends. Nor is it altogether envy of a skill the others do not possess. It is, instead, naked resentment: I alone appear to have progressed with my memoir, and they, or so I surmise, have been shamefully idle.

And here it may be pertinent to note that two of my three accusers are the very gentlemen already characterized in these pages as childish; and so, more and more manifestly, they are. As for the third offender, he is, shall we say, the kind of nonentity that follows the herd.

Same day, later. An architectural aside. I have alluded to the shutting of the Academy. The renovations that followed, in bringing about our present-day Temple House, required that four or five, and in one instance six, of these unheated cells be combined (i.e., razed) to create a single larger space to accommodate each new apartment. As a result, we now find ourselves in considerable comfort in the identical site of our early misery.

I ought also to add a word about the above-referenced library. The remodeling work necessitated the destruction of an area that from the earliest days of the Academy has always served as the headmaster's personal quarters, including the office to which pupils were summoned. It was in this sanctuary that Reverend Greenhill's library was kept. That it appeared as a bequest to the Trustees in his will was, it must be admitted, troublesome. Though his predecessors were piously, or let us say outwardly, celibate, Reverend Greenhill had come to us as a widower. He prided in his library as if (so goes the saying) it had sprung from his loins. It was his great pleasure and his even greater treasure. But to speak plainly, for the Trustees, at that time twenty-five strong and mainly men of business and law, what were we to do with these scores of volumes of theology and Greek and other such scholarly exotica? Of the several curators of the various institutes to which we offered this trove, all rejected it as an amateur's collection, hardly

unique and easily duplicated, much of it use-
lessly outdated. Today it is stored on dozens of
shelves in the kitchen pantry. Lately, I have been
leafing through a few of these old things, with
their curled and speckled pages, and in one, to
my delight and amazement, I discovered a paragraph naming Sir Flinders Petrie! I have since
removed this book (The Development of Palestine Exploration, by one Frederick Jones Bliss,
dated 1906) and display it here in my study, as
a suitable companion to my father's keepsakes. I
believe it would have pleased him to see it there.

*

June 26, 1949. Once again I have been reviewing these reflections, only to increase my
despondency. All is maundering, all is higgledy-
piggledy, nowhere do I find consecutive logic.
For this reason I have turned to my personal
copy of the History, hoping to come under its
superior influence. Unlike our present project,

this far more compendious work was composed by committee, with the benefit of a number of orderly minds contributing both to substance and style. It is in the spirit of research, in fact, that I am immersed in these crisply written chapters: I have sought to learn whether the Academy in its lengthening past has ever permitted the enrollment of Jewish pupils. A certain Claude Montefiore, of the English Montefiores, did attend in 1866, but only briefly, during his father's consular mission; but no others since, including up to my own father's time.

The absence of Jewish pupils, however, does not prevent the History from mentioning Jews, which it does fairly often, in general terms, with satirical or otherwise jesting comments on the Hebrew character. There is always, I believe, a kernel of truth in these commonplace disparagements. For instance, in my own Academy years I saw for myself how inbred is that notorious Israelite clannishness. Mr. Canterbury, as one would expect, held on to our traditional policy of exclusion, but with the coming of the Reverend Greenhill, some half-dozen or so Jewish boys were admitted, and I grew to know them well, if from a distance, lest I too be shunned. What was most remarkable about these unaccustomed newcomers, I observed, was not simply that they were Jews, or were said to be Jews, or acknowledged themselves (always diffidently) to be Jews. Yet in their appearance, and their ways, they were like everyone else: hardy on the football field (as I, incidentally, was not), hair dribbling over their eyes (a local fad), and in chapel yawning and restless and making faces, like the rest of us, at the departing Mr. Canterbury. Even their names were not noticeably distinctive, though one of them, Ned Greenhill, could scarcely have been related to Reverend Greenhill! This Ned, as it happens, and despite his effort to conceal it, was exceptional in Latin, becoming thereby a favorite of Reverend Greenhill, who held him up as a model. (An invidious rumor had it that Reverend Greenhill was privately tutoring him in Greek.) This alone was enough to encourage our avoidance, and anyhow these Hebrews did have the habit of clinging to their own. It has nevertheless since occurred to me that this unseemly huddling may have been the result, not the cause, of our open contempt. To speak to a Jew would be to lose one's place in our boyish hierarchy.

(Many years later, I would now and again lunch at the Oyster Bar with Ned Greenhill, by then a judge in the Southern District of New York. Our families, it goes without saying, never met.)

*

June 28, 1949. Upon my retirement from the law, I took away with me a very few objects evocative of my days and nights in that long-familar office, where my father and his father too had toiled: Miss Margaret Stimmer's machine, of course (with her permission), and also several small or middling items belonging originally to my grandfather, including a charming rocking-horse blotter made of green quartz, a weighty brass notary sealing device with its swan's-neck lever, and even a little bottle of India ink with a rubber stopper, once used to append indelible signatures to official documents. All these I still have with me here in my study, and a few, like the rocking-horse blotter and the India ink, I keep within daily sight on my writing table. (This ink, by the way, has never fully evaporated, thanks to its rubber stopper, and is as fluid as it was the day the bottle was first opened.) The reader may suppose that here I echo my father and his penchant for collecting; but this is hardly the case. All these oddments are quiet emblems of nostalgic reminiscence, whereas my father's things could mean nothing personal to him, being cryptic signals from an unknowable past. What can scratchings on the base of a beaker tell? If such an object does own a familial history, however remote, it is certainly not my father's.

It is possible, I presume, that this very beaker may carry his emotion in having once enjoyed a close association with Sir Flinders Petrie, and may stand as an expression of the altogether different life my father might have lived had he succumbed to temptation and continued in his cousin's path. If so, out of respect for my mother's memory, I cannot follow him there.

Thinking back, I am much moved to recall that the day I made Miss Margaret Stimmer's typewriter my own was the very day I permitted myself to call her Peg.

*

Fourth of July, 1949. The cell opposite mine (this was still within Mr. Canterbury's tenure), with the corridor between us, was for a long time unoccupied. The boy it belonged to had contracted tuberculosis, which for many weeks went unrecognized. There was much illness all around in those unbearably cold winter days, and our cells, as previously remarked, were unheated. Nearly everyone, the masters included, was subject to running noses and chronic coughing. Still, no one coughed with the vehemence and persistence of the pupil in the cell across from mine. I had no choice save to suffer through it; it kept me awake night after night. Mr. Canterbury was finally persuaded to inform the boy's guardian, who came and took him away. He never returned, and all we knew further of him was that a lawsuit was somehow involved. It was then that Mr. Canterbury disappeared from the Academy, and Reverend Greenhill arrived, and with him a welcome innovation: a feather quilt for each boy's bed. At the same time, he arranged for the halls to be heated (an amenity primitive by present standards); and one morning in chapel he instructed us to keep our doors open to let in the warmth, and also, he admonished, to invite the equal warmth of pleasant social discourse. (How odd to be remembering the cold, when the temperature today approaches 100 degrees!)

But soon another pupil lay in what had been the sick boy's bed. His door was often closed. Either he had come too late to be apprised of the new rule, or he chose to ignore it. Since he was in the form below mine, and attended different classes, I glimpsed him only intermittently, in the refectory or in chapel. His behavior in both these circumstances was odd. I never saw him eat a normal dinner. He seemed to live on bread and milk and hard-boiled eggs, and he always sat by himself. In chapel, even when reprimanded, he never removed his cap. In fact, I never saw him without it. And while the rest of us whispered and snickered and pretended to sneeze during the reading of the Gospel and all through the sermon, he seemed rigidly attentive. He joined in the singing of a certain few hymns, but for others he was willfully silent. In appearance he was also uncommon. He was so thin as to approach the skeletal (his legs were nearer to bone than flesh), and this I attributed to his sparseness of diet. His complexion was what

I believe is called olive, of the kind known to characterize the Mediterranean and Levantine peoples; but in contrast to this deficit of natural ruddiness, his hair was astoundingly red. And not the red of the Irish. As I write, I am put in mind of my father's description of the red earth of his days with Cousin William: deeper and denser and more otherworldly than any commonplace Celtic red.

He had come to us shortly after that influx of Jews, but he hardly seemed one of them, and they too, as we all did, were wary of everything about him, particularly his outlandish names, both the first and the last, which were all it was possible to know of him. There were some, playing on his surname, who joked that he was undoubtedly a Jew, given the elephantine length of his nose. To these jibes he said nothing, and merely turned away. And others (the more rowdy among us) claimed that only a Jew would flaunt Zion so brazenly, forgetting that the Psalms recited in chapel, which so frequently invoked Zion, were part and parcel of our Christian worship. I was particularly alert to this error, since on the Wilkinson side there can be found (too many, my father said) evangelical pietists who cling ardently to Zion, a few of whom are bizarrely devoted to speaking in tongues. And in the Petrie line too there have been numerous Old Testament appellations; we were once a sober crew of Abrahams and Nathans and Samuels, all of them proper Christians.

But there was more than Ben-Zion Elefantin's unusual name to irritate conventional expectations. Though rarely heard, his voice was perplexing. It had in it a pale echo of Mr. Canterbury's admirable vowels, but also an alien turn of the consonants, suggesting a combination of foreignisms—where exactly was he from? And why was he a full semester behind, in the form below mine, despite the fact, as I later learned, that at nearly twelve he was two years older than I? And was he mad, or merely a liar? I came, in time, to think the latter, though I was, I confess, something of a liar myself, feigning injuries of every variety in order to evade the football field. Mr. Canterbury had been inclined to expose me, and for punishment doubled my obligations to football and riding (like my father before me, I was greatly averse to horses); but Reverend Greenhill's view was that one's duty to God did not necessarily include kicking and galloping, and he sent me off to do as I pleased, as long as it harmed neither man nor beast.

What it pleased me to do during those football afternoons when the halls were deserted, and the shouting was distant and muffled, was to sit on my bed with my chessboard before me, while hoping to outwit a phantom opponent. On the memorable day I will now record, my door, according to protocol, was ajar, and when I looked up from my wooden troops, I saw Ben-Zion Elefantin standing there. Without speaking a word, he hopped on the bed to face me, and began maneuvering first a knight, and then a rook, and finally a queen, and I heard him say, very quietly, indeed humbly, If you don't mind, checkmate. I asked him then whether he, like me at that hour, had explicit permission to exempt himself from the field. He seemed to consider this for a moment, and said, with unhurried directness, I have no interest in that. I thought it was natural to inquire, since he was new to the Academy, in what other activity he did take interest. Chapel, he said. I found this unlikely; no boy I knew regarded chapel as anything other than a morning of aching tedium. Are you religious, I asked. The word does not apply, he said, at least not in the sense you intend. It was a strange way of speaking; no normal boy spoke like a book. I asked where he had been to school before coming to us. Oh, he said, many schools, in many places, but I never stay long, and until now was never taught fractions. Is that why, I asked, they've put you in fourth? Oh, he said, it hardly matters where I am put, before long they will call me away. Thank you, he said, for the pleasure of the game. And then he left me and went back to his room and shut the door.

July 5, 1949. Aside from yesterday's stifling weather (continuing at 97 degrees today), which compelled my breaking off my narrative too abruptly, the Fourth of July could not have been more disagreeable. A group of unruly youths from a neighboring town notorious for its shabbiness invaded our grounds, overturned the handsome old benches under the maples, and, targeting our windows, tossed deafening volleys of firecrackers while shouting obscenities. To such depths has patriotism fallen. Those warlike fumes have seeped into my study, where they hover still, stirred by useless electrical fans (I have two, and they do nothing to alleviate the abominable heat). One of the household staff, a half-incomprehensible native of Vienna, I suppose intending to please, made a pitiful attempt to celebrate the holiday by presenting us with what she calls a Sacher torte, an absurdly irrelevant cake of some kind, overly sugared; but one can expect nothing comfortably familiar from this postwar flotsam and jetsam. As for the disastrous war itself, our hard-won victory on two fronts is by now four years gone, yet there are some who even today decline to forgive President Roosevelt for, as they say, putting Americans at risk for the sake of saving the Jews. There may be, as always, the usual kernel of truth in this; but that the Jews weren't saved in any event (nor many others, for that matter) is proof of the overall purposelessness of that war. Hitler and Stalin, Tweedledum and Tweedledee. The newspapers are rife with grotesque tales of camps and ovens; one hardly knows what to believe, and I am nowadays drawn far less to these public contentions than to my own reflections. This is not to say that I am not proud of my son's participation in the war, though it lacked a certain manliness, I mean of exposure to danger, since he was never on the battlefield, but rather in a printing office—something to do with a publication for soldiers and sailors.

In connection with which, the reader will

have observed that save for her passing, I have
had little to say of my late dear wife, an avid
lover, as I earlier indicated, of the decorative arts;
I hope to correct this here. Yet Miranda's influence on our son was perhaps too pressing, and
may have led him to his current frivolous pre-
occupations in California. Miranda herself was
fond of such fanciful trivia, in the form of head-
ing the flower committee of her Women's Club
and numerous like pursuits, e.g., her accumula-
tion of painted bowls and porcelain figurines in
the Japanese style: a man in a flat hat drawing a
bucket out of a well, a sloe-eyed woman posed
on a bridge. More to the point, she was much
interested in the lives of Carole Lombard and
Myrna Loy, those so-called "stars" of cinema.
She liked to joke that I had married her only
because of her clear resemblance to Myrna Loy,
which was certainly not the case; at the time I
scarcely knew the name. Miranda was indeed
very pretty, but the reason for our marriage, of
which our son was the premature consequence,

remains entirely private. Nor can I deny that her parents insisted on it.

I see that I have again digressed, and though I mean to enlighten the reader further with regard to Ben-Zion Elefantin, I detect at this moment a relieving breath of a breeze beyond the sultry movements of the fans. The evening cool has begun, and I am off to walk in its respite. Yet first I must secure this manuscript before leaving my study. Until its completion I keep it for privacy in an unidentifiable box with a lid. It once held my father's cigars, and their old aroma lingers still.

★

July 6, 1949. A calamity, an outburst of childish spite. An inconceivable act of vengeance. It could not have been spontaneous; it had to have been carefully plotted, my habits noted, my comings and goings spied on. My colleagues have long been aware that at the close of these brutal equatorial days, I have taken to tracing the paths circling the maples, where wisps of evening airs rustle in their leaves. (Early this morning the staff, I am relieved to say, righted the benches and disposed of the debris, including a considerable scattering of beer bottles.)

At such times it is good to walk and think, walk and think. How am I to tell more of Ben-Zion Elefantin? I cannot reveal him in the way of dialogue (a practice my son puts his trust in, he informs me, as an aspiring screenwriter). I have not that gift or inclination. Nor am I certain it will finally be possible to reveal Ben-Zion Elefantin by any narrative device. It may be that all I knew of him was fabrication or delusion.

I wandered thusly, mulling these enigmas, for half an hour or so, and then returned to my study refreshed, intending despite the late hour to set down my thoughts. What I saw before me—saw in one hideous instant—was a scene of ghastly vandalism. On the surface of my writing table stood my little bottle of India ink, uncorked, with its rubber stopper prone beside it. Someone—someone!—had spilled its contents over the body of my Remington, obliterating the letters on its keys and wetting the roller so repulsively that it gleamed like some slithering black slime. Miss Margaret Stimmer's Remington violated, the very machine, now mine, once touched by her prancing fingers, and all I have left to remind me of my sweet Peg.

★

July 8, 1949. The reader will have noted that the foregoing paragraphs have been written, perforce, in longhand, and at various intervals, in various states of mind. Hedda of the kitchen staff (it was she who inspired the Sacher torte), seeing my distress, volunteered to take the despoiled Remington away in an attempt to clean it. She assured me that vinegar would do the job well enough, and so it mostly has, if not to my full satisfaction. The balls of my fingers still turn black from the keys, and the friction of typing sends up a fine mist of charcoal-like dust to coat my eyeglasses and nose. Hedda calms me with the promise that all this will not persist, and advises patience, or else a second vinegar bath. That the mechanism has not been irreparably harmed hardly assuages my shock: the assailant is one of us, a fellow Trustee!

I convened a meeting, not in my study as customary, but in the old chapel, with its reminder of the role of conscience in life. My purpose was to initiate a small facsimile of trial by jury, every man on his honor. Each of my six colleagues denied any malfeasance, but no one more vociferously than our nonagenarian, on whose collar and sleeve I had noticed some minute signs of spatter. Of course, he replied, what do you expect of a fountain pen when you inadvertently press too hard on its point? Why am I alone to be named culpable, when all, excepting yourself, write with ordinary pen and ink, as men of authority usually do? Only you, he went on, conduct yourself no better than a female office hireling, racketing away into the night.

It was that "female" that was particularly wounding: was it a barb at Miss Margaret Stimmer? Apparently our friendship had escaped not a few. And so, since the others unanimously supported the likely culprit's deflecting hypothesis (and I am sorry to say that further discussion deteriorated into a vigorous comparison of fountain pen brands, whether the Parker is actually superior to the Montblanc, etc.), my effort to secure justice and truth came to nothing.

*

July 12, 1949. I no longer walk in the evenings (and besides, the paths are precariously littered with splintered branches), and have come to a certain understanding with myself. I will not permit the hurtful hostility of others to undermine what moves me. This was a lesson I learned in boyhood, when on account of my growing

interest in Ben-Zion Elefantin I too became
persona non grata. Our early initiation into a
mutual liking of chess was bound to turn public,
with my door always open in compliance with
Reverend Greenhill's instruction. No wonder
our venture took on an aspect of the conspirato-
rial: whispered notions of when it was best to
be free of the herd, or too abruptly quitting the
refectory, first one, and then the other. On two
or three weekday occasions, as I painfully recall,
when we had found refuge in the vacant chapel, we were discovered and mocked, Ben-Zion
Elefantin for his name and his incomprehensible
origin, and I for my intimacy with so freakish
a boy.

I speak too easily of intimacy; it was slow
in coming, and was never wholly achieved. He
was unnatural in too many ways. The abundance of his uncut hair, for instance: not only
its earth-red yet unearthly color, but what I sus-
pected might be a pair of long curls sprouting
from the temples, each one hidden behind an ear

and lost in the overall mass. Through his shut
door (he never obeyed any principle he disliked)
I would sometimes hear the rise and fall of foreign mutterings, morning and evening, as if he
were quietly growling secret incantations. There
were times when, both of us fatigued by too
many battles of knights and bishops, he would
sit silent and staring, having nothing to say, and
waiting for me to signal some subject of merit.
I told him of Mr. Canterbury's terrible reign,
and how he ought to be glad to have missed it,
and of the visit the previous year from Pelham,
a nearby town, of an elderly Mr. Emmet, one of
the Temple cousins, hence also cousin to Henry
James, whose portrait hung in the chapel. To
have Mr. Emmet in our midst, however briefly
(he spent but an hour or two), was considered
a privilege: he had once enjoyed an afternoon's
colloquy with Henry James Senior, the nov-
elist's father, when the philosopher Emerson,
who happened also to be present, shook Mr.
Emmet's hand, and asked him how he was, and

made some comment on the charms of Concord, delighting Mr. Emmet with his attentions. For us, we were advised, great fame attached itself to Mr. Emmet's very flesh: his was the hand that the philosopher's hand had honored.

Emmet, Temple, James: all these local references, so dear to the Academy's history, and passed fervently on to its pupils, left Ben-Zion Elefantin indifferent; but the mention of Canterbury roused him in a way I had never before witnessed, and he told me that it was one of the places he had been to school, and where he first learned to read English. Of all languages, he said, the language of English people was his favorite, and though he had been put in school in Canterbury for only a few weeks, and was soon taken away to Frankfurt and afterward Rome, he fell permanently into the sea of their stories, Mary Lamb's Tales from Shakespeare and The Old Curiosity Shop and Ivanhoe and Robinson Crusoe and Adam Bede, books I had barely heard of and would never care to read, as he did, on his own, and have never read since. He told all this as if in confidence, as if he trusted me not to disclose it, as if to disclose it would increase what he believed to be his peril. He seemed to me pitiful then, with his unnatural hair and unnatural voice, which I all at once heard not so much as stilted but as somehow mysteriously archaic, or (I hardly know my own meaning as I tell this) uncannily ancestral. Too many cities were in his tones, and I argued that no one can come from everywhere, everyone must come from somewhere, and where specifically was he from? He thanked me again for our several tournaments and crossed the hall and again shut his door.

I was by now used to such opacities, and scarcely minded them, having other annoyances to trouble me, chiefly my lost status. I was, after all, a Petrie, and a Petrie by nature belongs to the mockers, not to the mocked. I sometimes thought of reversing my lot by joining in the ridicule of Ben-Zion Elefantin; but I quickly learned, after a single attempt, that it could not be done: once an outcast, always an outcast. And more: the humiliation I felt in my inability to recover my standing was small in comparison to the flood of shame that unexpectedly overtook me in having momentarily betrayed Ben-Zion Elefantin. As for the jibes, in time they diminished (I had observed Reverend Greenhill summon the worst of our tormentors for a talk), and in their place we were mutely snubbed like a pair of invisible wraiths. But it freed us from hiding, and since no one would speak to either of us, and Ben-Zion Elefantin had little to say to me, we were anyhow thrown together under a carapace of unwilling quiet. In the refectory I sat close to him with my full dinner plate before me as he carefully drew out the yolk from his single egg. And the same in chapel, when I could sense from my nearness to his breathing how tensely he listened to the readings of Scripture.

On a certain morning of fine weather when Exodus was the theme of Reverend Greenhill's sermon, and the rout of the Egyptians was under moral consideration (whether so massive a drowning of men and horses was too wrathful a punishment even for oppressors), Ben-Zion Elefantin for the first time made himself known to me. A three-hour Sunday afternoon recess had been declared: another of Reverend Greenhill's ameliorating innovations, where formerly Mr. Canterbury had enforced a Sabbath study period of the same length, to be conducted in strictest silence. On this day of freedom, while our classmates were out on the sunny lawns, tossing balls and aimlessly running and blaring their laughter to the skies, Ben-Zion Elefantin and I sat on my bed as usual, with my chessboard between us. But the game was somehow desultory, and on an impulse, remembering the morning's sermon and the strange profundity of his attentiveness, I told him that I owned some actual things from the time of the Pharaohs, whether he could believe me or not. My father, before I was born, I said, was once in Egypt, when my mother was too ill to go with him, but still he brought back for her a gold Egyptian ring, which for some reason she never wore. I said I had often seen the ring in the pretty bowl on her dresser along with her necklaces and bracelets, but it interested me far less than the other things my father had come home with, and if he didn't believe me that they were really from Egypt, I could show them to him. I had never before spoken to anyone of what lay hidden in the pouch in the cabinet under my table, and the reader may question why I did so now. A kind of agitation seemed to possess him, and I saw that his face was burning bloodlike, nearly the color of his hair. You know nothing of Egypt, he said, nothing, you think everything in the Bible is true, but there is more than the Bible tells, and omission is untruth. (I am trying to render the queer way of his speech, how the suddenness of its heat turned it old and ornate, as if he was not a boy but a fiery ghost in some story.) I'll show you, I said, and what makes you think you know more about Egypt than my own father, who really was there, and went down the Nile in a boat, and was close to Sir Flinders Petrie, his cousin, an expert on everything Egyptian, and do you even know who Sir Flinders Petrie is? He said he did not, but neither would Sir Flinders Petrie, whoever he was, know the truth of Ben-Zion Elefantin. This took me aback; how stupid you sound, I said, and he gave me an answer both triumphal, as in an argument he was bound to win, and also despairing, as if he was conscious of how I would receive it. I myself, he said, was born in Egypt, and lived there until it was time for my schooling. I was instantly doubtful: hadn't my father in his notebook described the Egyptians as dusky? And in pictures of pyramids and palms and such weren't Egyptians always shown to be copper-colored? Certainly no Egyptian had hair the color of red earth. You can't be Egyptian, I said. Oh, he said, I am not Egyptian at all. But if you were born in Egypt and aren't Egyptian, I asked, what are you? Then I saw something like a quiver of fear pass over his eyelids. I am Elefantin, he said, and he

July 19, 1949. It has been more than a week since I was made to break off, and I have since not had the heart to come back to my Remington. At that time, as it happened, I had been typing at three in the afternoon, and I hope the reader will not be tempted to think that I had altered my midnight labors out of cowardice, to accommodate my accusers. No, it was because I was driven to go on, my memories racked me, and though three was most often the hour when I helplessly succumbed to a doze, with the fans struggling against the heat, still I could not contain my feeling, stirred as I was by my retelling of Ben-Zion Elefantin's unimaginable words (which I have yet to record). So inwardly gripped was I, that I was altogether deaf to the voices that wafted through the open window, until I was distracted by an unwelcome tumult of loud and offensive laughter. In some exasperation I looked out to see its source. My six colleagues were lazily gathered under the maples, a sign that they were hardly at work on their memoirs. One of them, his arm in the air, appeared to be pointing upward, directly at my window, and then the laughter erupted again. It was, not surprisingly, that childish cackling old man, the spiteful culprit himself, the vandal, the despoiler of my Remington. He stood with his walker before him, and, having caught my eye, stepped forward with the start of a salute, as if about to wave in ill-intended greeting. And then—I knew it seconds before—a broken branch under his feet—he had been looking up and never saw it. He tottered for an instant and lurched downward, his legs snarled in the legs of the walker, and fell in a twisted heap of elderly limbs. I was witness to all of it, the shrieking and calling, Hedda and two or three others of the staff all at once there, warning and herding the others out of the way, five stricken old men, and then the ambulance with its distant siren, and the police and the gurney, and my enemy was taken away. He died in the hospital six days later (yesterday), not, they say, from the fractured hip or the surgery or the infamously inevitable pneumonia that set in soon after, but from, they say, heart failure. And Hedda tells me, with some contempt, that one of the kitchen help believes it was I who destroyed him, I with my evil eye. A foolish superstition, yet I feel its vengeful truth.

We were seven, and now we are six. I think incessantly of death, of oblivion, how nothing lasts, not even memory when the one who remembers is gone. And how can I go on with my memoir, to what end, for what purpose? What meaning can it have, except for its writer? And for him too (I mean for me), the past is mist, its figures and images no better than faded paintings. Where now is Ben-Zion Elefantin, did he in fact exist? Today he is no more than an illusion, and perhaps he was an illusion then?

As for the dead man, I cannot mourn. How can I mourn the envious boor who wounded my sweet Peg? Still, there is a kind of mourning in the air, the gloom seeps and seeps, one feels the breath of a void, not only of a missing tenant of Temple House (him I cannot mourn) but of the limitless void that awaits us. The tremor in my left hand has lately worsened. When I shave, the leathern creature in the mirror is someone I do not know, and too often I draw blood from his living flesh, if flesh it is. Hedda reports that the afternoon tea trays, all save mine, are sent back untouched. And more: she tells me that the other one, that other puerile fellow, the dead man's inseparable accomplice and defender, sits all day in his apartment and weeps. But I cannot forget that when my enemy stood pointing and jeering at my window, the laughter of his steady companion was the loudest. (So much for the delicate syllables of their precious Gerard Manley Hopkins.)

*

July 20, 1949. I have decided, after all, to continue with my memoir. Too many reflections on death contaminate life. And should not each man live every day as if he were immortal? After all this time, I cannot proceed from where I left off: let those broken words hang cryptic and unfinished while I describe my surprise at Ben-Zion Elefantin's indifference to my father's treasure. With the exception of the notebook, I had emptied the pouch of all its objects, one by one, and set them out in a row on my table. I say his indifference, but since his turmoil was unabated, I should rather say contempt. You suppose these things to be uncommon, he said, on account of what you believe to be their ancient age, but your father may have been gullible, as so many are. They can be found by the hundreds, real and false. My parents would know. They know such things with their fingertips. My father, I protested, wasn't gullible, and why should your parents know more than my father, who brought them back from Egypt? My father, I told you, worked in Giza with Sir Flinders Petrie, his very own cousin, and Sir Flinders Petrie isn't gullible, he knows more about Egypt than anyone. He coughed out a small gurgling noise that I took to be a scoff, and then his voice too became small and quiet and more foreign than ever. My parents, he said, are traders.

Even as a boy of ten I understood what a trader was. My father, I had seen, was every morning absorbed by stocks and bonds, and followed them in the newspapers, and besides, according to what I took in from his talk, I knew that traders lived in Wall Street, not in legendary places like Egypt. All this I explained to Ben-Zion Elefantin. And after this conversation he had no more to say, and I was glad that I had not yet revealed to his certain scorn, as I had at first intended, what I imagined to be my father's dearest prize, the emerald-eyed beaker in its box under my bed. A misunderstanding had come between us, or was it a quarrel, and why? He left me and went to his room and again shut the door, and for all the next week he kept away.

★

July 21, 1949. The reader will, I trust, understand why I must eke out my memoir in these unsatisfying patches. In part it is simple fatigue. The tremor in my left hand has somehow begun to assert itself in my right hand as well, hence my typing becomes blighted by too many errors, which I must laboriously correct. After an hour or so at my Remington I feel called upon to lie down, and invariably this leads to a doze. I will confess to another cause of hiatus upon hiatus, and here I admit also to a growing sympathy for my colleagues, who, it is clear, have achieved little or nothing beyond an initial paragraph or two, if even that. As I move on with my chronicle, I more and more feel an irrepressible ache of yearning, I know not for what. Hardly for my boyhood in the Academy, with all its stringencies and youthful cruelties. I am, if I may express it so, in a state of suffering of the soul as I write, a suffering that is more a gnawing paralysis than a conscious pain. I earnestly wish to stop my memoir, and I may not, so how can I blame those others who have stopped, or not so much as begun? I fear that I am again in the grip of the void. All around me the talk is of the accident under the maples, and how it came about, and of broken branches, and the terror of falling. Nor am I immune from that terror, and see anew the wisdom of my having given up my meditative if lonely evening walks in the perilous paths beneath the trees. I think of the loneliness I felt in my childhood, which returns to me now, as if all loneliness, past and present, were one. To be shunned in the company of Ben-Zion Elefantin was painful enough (after all, we had each other), but to endure, all on my own, the snubs and the silences of those persecutors who had once been my peers, was another.

Then how relieved and grateful I was when the following Sunday he came to sit quietly beside me in chapel (where the pew had been spitefully left unoccupied to my right and my left), as if he meant to forgive me for what he deemed to be my fault. And when at last we were set free from the tiresome readings and hymns (the sermon that day was from Matthew), with no discussion of any kind he led me not to my room but to his, and we sat on his bed facing each other as always, though with no chessboard between us, and his door shut as always. His room was nearly identical to mine, the bed as narrow, the walls as bare, the ceiling as stained: a monklike cubicle reminiscent, yes, of a prisoner's cell. Still, a certain surprising difference was instantly noticeable. I kept a stack of books on my table, all of them schoolbooks: my History of the World, my Beginner's Algebra, my (hated) Gallic Wars, and so forth; but here his table was altogether clear of any evidence of schooling, as if he meant to wash away all signs of it, except for a fourth-form Intermediate Arithmetic, with its bruised and faded binding, tossed to the floor among gray clumps of wandering dust. (It was plain that he had chosen not to obey the requirement of cleaning one's own room.)

Yet his table held a panoply of perplexing

items: a drawstring sack of some fine material, silk or satin, and next to it a pair of small black cubes, or were they boxes, attached to what appeared to be twin leather leashes, rather like a pony's reins. And lying open beside this eerie contraption, a distinctly foreign-looking book. Its blackened corners were frayed, and an unknown odor drifted faintly from it, like the smell, I imagined, of some forest fungus. I saw that its letters were unrecognizable, and asked whether he could actually read such ugly blotches, and what language was that? He said nothing at first, as if deciding whether to answer, and then shut the book and opened the drawer of his table and carefully deposited it there, meanwhile maneuvering the contraption with its curly reins into its sack before positioning this too, again delicately, into that same hidden place. It is very old, this language, he said finally, and I must now apologize to you. You could not know, he said, how could you know, no one ever knows, they suppose this and that, or they think I speak foolishness, and why should I have expected that you, unlike all others, would understand? His voice shook, and also his hands. Perhaps, he said, it is that I believed you to be my friend, and now I am ashamed. I *am* your friend, I said, and was all at once frightened by my own words, as if I might really be speaking truth. To be the friend of a grotesquerie (this fearsome term comes to me only now) seemed far more dangerous than the boyish pariahship that was already my plight. The peril worsened: he slid off his end of his bed and pulled me down beside him, with his face so close to mine that I could almost see my eyes in the black mirror of his own. I had never before felt the heat of his meager flesh; sitting side by side in the chapel's confining pews, our shoulders in their Academy blazers had never so much as grazed—nor had our knees in our short trousers. And now, the two of us prone on the floor among the nubbles of dust, breathing their spores, I seemed to be breathing his breath. Our bare legs in the twist of my fall had somehow become entangled, and it was as if my skin, or his own, might at any moment catch fire. He spoke with a rhythmic rapidity, almost as if he were reciting, half by rote, some time-encrusted liturgical saga. It had no beginning, it promised no end, it was all fantastical middle, a hallucinatory mixture of languages and implausible histories. And what was I, pressed body to body, to make of it?

The attentive reader (if by now such reader there be) is my witness; only see how I have too long put off the telling of it, and how can I tell it even now, when in fulfillment of my memoir I must? Can I reach out my fingers to capture a cloud, a vapor, an odor? Then do not think that I own the power to replicate any graspable representation of what came to pass that afternoon in my tenth year, when the shouts from the football field were themselves no more than some distant ghostly abrasion. Nevertheless, insofar as my feeble understanding under these circumstances will permit, I will attempt to extract

from Ben-Zion Elefantin's untamed babblings a
semblance of human coherence. As I say, I must
try. But no, it cannot be done; not by me, and
who else is there? No other person on earth, and
this damnable tremor begins to rock my wrists,
my fatigue defeats me, the keys of my Remington are no better than boulders, I fear a panic
will soon overtake me if I do not stop, and here
thank God is Hedda with the supper tray thank
God thank God thank God

3:30 AM

Sleep has eluded me for many hours, so deep
is my abashment. To have lost self-possession,
and to such a degree, in the presence of the
kitchen help! And that Hedda should have seen
me so disheveled, with my shirt collar wet, and
these shaming infantile tears, how am I different
from that forsaken miscreant whom in my private mind I call the Childish One? What is it to

me that he mourns his misbegotten accomplice? And what is it Hedda must think? Two old men weeping, two old men grieving? I myself hardly know why I grieve, and for whom? For my unhappy boyhood, for my sweet Peg, for my unlucky and frivolous son? And to find me so undone, and yet to have come with her own lament! Two of the staff have departed, she told me, without a word of warning, and how was she to cope, she and that slattern Amelia, das Flittchen, only the two of them, diese Schlümpfe lazy and useless, left in charge of six broken old men, each more zerbrechlich than the next, the frailest of all starving himself night and day on his dirty sofa with his head down, refusing to eat a crumb of bread or sip a drop of tea, a sick man who ought to be in the hospital? And who was to get him there? Did he have a wife, a daughter, a son? What was she to do with him? What was I, in my capacity as Trustee, to do with him, has he no family, no friend, no heir?

I replied that I would review the Charter of

the Trust to determine a suitable course, and then, unable to look her in the eye, I dismissed her.

*

July 22, 1949. Further to the Charter. The original, of course, is in the Academy vault at J. P. Morgan, but I retain a copy here in my study, where I keep it together with my personal volume of the History, though I have rarely consulted it since the establishment of Temple House, when additional clauses were necessarily incorporated. And indeed there is provision for such a contingency as care for the seriously moribund, the funding for which to come under the bank's jurisdiction. Setting all this in motion, alas, falls to me. It cannot escape my judgment that this childless miscreant's predicament is no better than that of a vagrant found dying in the street; yet I who have a son, will my own fate differ when I too inevitably succumb?

It has now been several weeks, in fact I

count two months, since I have had any word from my son. In light of the length of this period of silence, I will confess to having broken a wary and unacknowledged vow (unacknowledged by him, wary on my side). I mean by this that rather than wait for his own action in this respect, I undertook to telephone him, in part because I believe his resources are, as usual, low, and in the hope of sparing him the expense of a long-distance call. The result was unfortunate, and I am largely, if unintentionally, to blame. Though I have not spoken of it outright, I presume it is fully evident that given my retirement, and with no further Petrie to carry the firm on into the future (my son having preferred a less onerous path), the venerable Petrie partnership is now lamentably defunct. On this occasion, despite my long-held familiarity with time-zone vagaries—a mere one-hour difference from Chicago, three from Los Angeles, and what law office can function without such instinctive knowledge—my memory abandoned me and caused an unforgivable intrusion: I reached my son in the middle of his California night. He was, I admit, startled, and reminded me that this unexpected disruption was not my first such malfeasance; it had happened twice before. I felt constrained to apologize, which only brought on a kind of confusion, or rather anger, on his part: he explained that he and a collaborator were working through the night on content (his strange jargon) which may have already interested a producer. I believe this is what he told me. Or was it that the producer was at that very moment at his side? Certainly he was not alone; I heard what I took to be a nearby voice, a murmur that was kin to laughter.

These increasing forgettings greatly distress me, and perhaps the ingenious inventors of our modern era, who have already brought us the television sets that are beginning to proliferate even beyond the barroom, will one day devise a telephone that allows one to know the identity of the caller before responding. Such a development would surely inhibit my son's growing coolness, and my embarrassment at discovering him in flagrante delicto.

*

July 25, 1949. What has become of me? Excess emotion has made me shameless, and my tongue (I mean my prose) is paralyzed by coarse legalisms. A memoir ought not to be a deposition, and how I wish it were, with all its conciseness and clarity. Instead, I write, indeed I speak, in turbulence, captive of these helpless tears that terrify me, as if I am already blundering in the haze and corrosions of a dying brain. Was it some crackpot seizure of dream and dementia that took hold of me four days ago when I *could not* summon Ben-Zion Elefantin's deposition, if that is what he meant it to be, his pleading a case for his curious existence, his pitiful defense? How can I find my way out of this wilderness of hesitation? Or dare I say shame?

. . .

5:21 AM. Dawn. My wrists, my very ribs, ache from the keys. Longhand no better. A spilled vessel. Drowned. As if strangled by trance. The voice is not mine. Then whose? And how?

★

July 26, 1949. Here I must explain a change I am introducing in the organization of the admittedly chaotic document presently under my hand. It will be recalled that as these pages accumulated, I at one time stored them in a rectangular box (it once sheltered my father's substantial Cuban cigars) with an ornamental lid, the lid to serve as a warning to trespassers. But the growing length of my memoir can no longer be contained in so shallow a receptacle, and in any event I no longer fear a recurrence of vandalism: the vandal is dead. (Sans gravestone, it pleases me to say. Through Hedda I learn that the nonagenarian's younger brother, himself a fading octogenarian, has disposed of the ashes in some obscure upstate waterway.) Hence I am free now to allow these increasing pages to build as they will, open to sight and secured by a cherished paperweight: my grandfather's antiquated brass notary seal. The vacant box will henceforth have another use. I intend to sequester therein a certain portion of this manuscript, i.e., what I can only describe as my attempt to transcribe the tenor of Ben-Zion Elefantin's utterances. Not, let it be understood, that they have faded over the last seven or more decades. On the contrary: they remain for me akin to a burning bush, unquenchable. I will determine later whether I judge this putative transcription to be suitable or worthy (I mean comprehensible). If not, and it is the crux of my memoir, then all that I have set down so far will be null and void. But even if it should have a certain validity, ought it to be preserved? Or does it demand to be hidden, lest it expose an already broken being, one whom

I once loved (while unaware of that love) and whose whereabouts today I do not know?

*

[Note: concealed herein are the papers in question. As of this writing, August 2, 1949, they will so remain until their disposition is determined, which determination will itself depend on the trustworthiness of the contents.]

You asked how I came here to the Academy. My uncle brought me. In every city where my parents are obliged to leave me, there is always an uncle to choose a school for me, yet not one of them is truly an uncle. How my present uncle happened on this place, it is impossible to surmise. It may be that he was impressed by what he took to be a congenial name, and believed that my parents might be pleased by it. My father and mother are transients and travelers, with no settled home, they are buyers and sellers, they are seekers and doubters, and they live mainly in hotels. Some of these hotels are pleasant, most are not, but rather than being shut up in a school, I always prefer those indifferent rooms where we never stay long and I am never expected to explain who I am, or pressed to find a friend my own age. When I was much younger, I pleaded to be taken wherever they might go, and promised that I would never complain of the heat or cry if I hated the food, and would never be sick, and would always be good. But they told me there were too many dangers for a child in those Levantine regions of constant upheaval where their particular business led them. To calm me, they explained as simply as they could that though they held themselves out to be ordinary traders, they were in truth pilgrims in search of a certain relic of our heritage, and that this was the primary hope of their work. Somewhere, I came to understand, lying unrecognized in one of the thousand alleyways and souks in the village markets of Egypt, or Palestine, or Syria, or Iraq, this significant thing, whatever it was, could be uncovered.

And when I asked why it was significant, they assured me that one day, when I was older, I would see for myself, and meanwhile, until it was found, they must earn our bread. This, they said, was the reason for their peregrinations: it was for the sake of foreign objects, exceedingly ancient, that persons in the West coveted and might wish to buy. And when I asked why these objects were coveted, my father replied It is for the vanity of the coveters, and my mother said It is because they are hollow and have no histories of their own. This was the cause of our having come to New York, where there are many such buyers. Our hotel in this city was too small and too cramped and too noisy, near streets made too bright in the middle of the night and crowds swimming like fishes all around, but still I would be more content to be left in such an unsavory scene than confined here where there are grasses and trees and schoolbooks without interest or weight, and where Scripture, the story of my people, is derided and whistled at by unlettered boys. My parents are not to blame, they must leave me behind to purchase their wares from fellahin who scratch with their hoes among the stones of the field, or from hawkers who crook their fingers under the shadowy arches of defeated cities. And soon an uncle will come to take me away to another hotel in another country, where a different uncle will accompany me to another school.

What my parents promised has come to pass. Though the significant thing has yet to be discovered, I have by now seen for myself who we are. My family name reveals our origins, which for reasons of rivalry and obfuscation have been omitted from the

Books of the Jews, where it ought by historic
rights to have been set within the chronicles
of the Israelites. Never mind that there are
in our own language missives attesting to
our presence—we Elefantins remain outcasts
from the history of our people. They say of
us that because of our far-flung island home
we were without knowledge of the breadth of
the imperatives of Moshe our Teacher, whom
we revered, and followed into the wilderness.
As if we are not ourselves Israelites, as if we
too did not stand at Sinai among the multi-
tudes of the Exodus! If it is true that we have
been erased from Torah, it is because we are
victims of falsifying scholars, betrayers who
have become our interpreters. They have
written of us as servile mercenaries, willing
sentries for the haughty Persians who over-
ran Egypt and commanded a fort to fend off
yet other invaders—but are they not themselves mercenaries in the pay of the lies of the
scholars? We, the Elefantins, hold our own

truths. Our traditions and practices are far weightier than the speculations of those ignorant excavators, those papyrologists who pollute our ruined haven with their inventions and prevarications. Of our truth they make legends. Hirelings on behalf of the Persian conquerors of Egypt we never were! With our generations of loam-red hair, Nubians and Egyptians we are not. Rather we are what our memories tell us, lost stragglers, dissenters who became separated in the wilderness from that mixed throng of snivelers after the fleshpots of our persecutors. We alone were unyieldingly faithful to Moshe our Teacher, we alone never succumbed to their foolish obeisance to a gilded bovine of the barnyard. Willingly we parted from them, and blundered our way we knew not where, and in the scalding winds of the desert hardly discerned north from south, or east from west. In the innocent blindness of our flight we turned back to an Egypt ruled now not by pharaohs but by foreign overlords, a green island inhabited by idolators who there had built a temple to Khnum, a fantastical god of the Nile in the ludicrous shape of a ram, and yet another god with the limbs of a man and the head of a stork, and still other gods of the river, red-legged storks that they mummified to preserve their divinity. And for their rites and libations they fashioned slender vessels made in the image of storks. All the gods of the nations are ludicrous, and all are fantastical, all but the Creator of All who created all the suns and their planets, and all the rivers and seas of the earth. And because we had no fear of the imaginings they called their gods, who for lack of existence could not have ordered the fullness and withdrawal of the Nile, we built, very near to their fraudulent shrine, our Temple to the Creator of All. It was in this way that we came as true Israelites to Elephantine.

These were the beliefs and writings and

precepts of the heritage I received from my father and my mother, who had received the very same from their predecessors, as they in turn had received them from our distant progenitors who raised up the Temple at Elephantine. Since then, we have been as a people scattered and few, and worse: forgotten, as if we never were. We live on as if in hiding. Even when our Temple stood, how humble it was, and how it disdained grandeur! It was built low to the earth, and constructed of earth, with a modest courtyard and fine tiles on its floor, and never a pillar blooming with crests of stone flora. We were, after all, stragglers. It was not our fate to go up to Jerusalem, or to set eyes on the stream that is called Jordan. Our companionate river was the Nile, once divinely bloodied so that we as a wretched people could escape our condition as slaves. It was through our proximity to the watery site of these memories that the Passover remains precious to us—and still we are expelled from the Books of the Jews!

And then, in a turn of our fortune, it was revealed to us by certain travelers that on a summit in the town of Jerusalem there was still another Temple, this one very grand, and peopled by Priests and Levites, to whom letters were sent, and from whom letters arrived. They too spoke and wrote our language, as who among the nations did not? In their inquiries we saw that though we may have been acknowledged as fellow Israelites, we were also regarded as improbable curiosities: they wished to know how we lived, how our families and neighbors were constituted, what our usages were, what plants and beasts and fowl there were on our island, and much else. We told them of the rich moisture of our reddish clay, how sheep and cattle were few while birds were many, especially the storks that thrived in colonies in the shallows of the Nile; and at first they made no murmurings against our Temple. And little by little, as we informed them of our beginnings and our ways, we learned theirs: the history of how their Temple was ruined, and how they were exiled to Babylon, and how they returned to rebuild it, all under the rule of the very Persians for whom we were supposedly abject hirelings! They told us of their commandments and ordinances, written in the books we stragglers did not possess, they told us of the Book of their teachers Ezra and Nehemiah, and their Book of holy instructions called Dvarim. And according to the wisdom of these books, they believed that only their Temple on the heights of Jerusalem permitted worship of the Creator of All, and that all other sanctums were forbidden, inclined as they were to the ludicrous and fantastical gods of the nations, and to false icons of gold and licentious figurines. And so it was according to the wisdom of these books that our riverine Temple, so contagiously close to the delusionary shrine of Khnum, was soon deemed illicit. But was not our Temple, like theirs, adorned by a seven-branched menorah, and a shulchan for the shewbread, and did not our kohanim, like theirs, honor the rites of sacrifice, were not birds brought by our people as burnt-offerings, all the birds that were pure, and none, like the stork, that were not? And was not our Temple also razed by enemies, our neighbors the priests of Khnum, who hated us because we doubted their gods? And were we too not exiled from our soil and compelled to sojourn elsewhere? We who revered Moshe our Teacher and faithfully followed him into the wilderness and never made obeisance to a gilded bovine of the barnyard!

It is through these commandments and ordinances that we have been made to disappear. And so we live on as apparitions, fearful of mockery. And I, Ben-Zion Elefantin, am just such an apparition, am I not?

*

August 3, 1949. Oh my feelings, my feelings! How they drive me, not since the passing of my darling, my Peg, my own sweet Peg, never since then, and I scarcely know why. My father's box here on my desk a veritable oven, the words within burn and burn, indeed they smell of clinging smoke, I begin to fear they are counterfeit, contraband of my own making, my brain is dizzied, I am not myself, we are under a violent tropical heat breathing fire, 103 degrees on this the second brutal day of it, the fans vanquished, a cosmic furnace where sanity wants nothing more than ice water, and this foolish woman chooses to cook her Saftgoulasch! She comes to me panting, with a red face and the sweat flooding her neck, to give me news of that feckless pair of kitchen defectors, and to complain yet again how doubly hard the work is for her without the men to do the heavy labor, is she expected to lift barrels? And das Flittchen Amelia, she is for spite schtum (when excited Hedda loses hold of her English), she knows three days already where they go, ein hochnäsige restaurant making bigger its business where are so many trains and in this bitter house so much work and Mäuse in the pantry and that old man sick in his head crying crying stinking of his own kacken, wie lang müssen wir noch auf diese verehrte Finanziere und ihre blöden Papiere warten?

And so forth. I told her that the mills of the bankers grind slowly, and what leads her to think that in such miserable heat any normal man could get that greasy damn stew down his gullet, and as for the mainstay of the staff going off to wait tables in the city, no wonder the rats are leaving the sinking ship, so why not the Oyster Bar in preference to this waning mice-ridden edifice?

Hedda is a respectable woman. I have never before quarreled with her. I have never thought to offend her.

★

August 5, 1949. Relief. After four detestable days, that hellish heat wave has broken. Hedda has begun to speak to me again, though I never did eat her stew. As for the Oyster Bar's coming to mind, I believe it must have been some considerable time before my retirement that Ned Greenhill and I last lunched there. It was convenient for both of us, my office just around the corner from Grand Central, and the Courthouse downtown, ten minutes by subway. In homage to the name, Ned habitually ordered oysters, while I, mindful of my nervous digestion, kept to milder flounder. The place in those days had its own confidential dimness. A couple of fellows could sit with their drinks in a semblance of seclusion, while up and down the ramp the plebs ran for their trains. I remember how the tables vibrated with the underground scrapings of wheels on rails. A pity, all this remodeling and refurbishing and hiring of new staff. Nowadays every comfortable old space submits to this fad of architectural vastness, every public room a modernist boast. Happily the Academy escaped this destiny when it was metamorphosed into

Temple House, though perhaps too many of the original Oxonian genuflections were retained. (I mean those fortresslike gray turrets that some of the upper-form rowdies claimed were in need of condoms.) Casual reminiscences such as these began our infrequent meetings, but after several glasses of wine we ventured, on the occasion I allude to, into more personal exchanges. I might insert here that Ned is careful never to speak of his son, I suspect out of consideration of me, since I have so little to say of mine. Unlike many of his kind, he is no braggart, especially in view of his own success. (I see in the Times that he is currently being sought after for an appellate appointment.) At Harvard he studied philosophy with one Harry Wolfson, a luminary unfamiliar to me, but well known, Ned made clear, to Reverend Greenhill—at least to his library, as I lately saw for myself. (I regret to say that I also saw rodent droppings all along the shelves.) Ned's memories of our long-ago headmaster have often dominated our conversations: Rever-

end Greenhill's amusement at the similarity of
their family names coexisting with the dissimi-
larity of their ancestry, his eagerness to intro-
duce Ned to the understanding of Greek, and his
general favoritism toward Ned, unluckily making him the butt of his classmates.

At his mention of this word, I asked whether
he recalled an undersized and taciturn fourth-
form boy with a farcical pachyderm name, which
everyone ridiculed. I said this jokingly, and
almost dismissively, so as not to reveal my
ardent interest in what he might tell me. Oh
yes, he said, who could forget such an oddity,
myself in particular, since I too was mocked, and
worse than mocked, along with the other Jewish boys, but in my case all the more so because
Reverend Greenhill had singled me out. It was
not only for the pleasure he took in my being
drawn to the classical languages, rare enough in
the Academy, he told me, but also because he
had observed my restraint when bullied, and
believed I might understand this boy's irregular

situation, and would be willing to befriend him. No former headmaster had agreed to take in a pupil sent over from the Elijah Foundation, and Canterbury his predecessor had insisted on its improbability on grounds of proper religion. I was curious to know what was the nature of such a Foundation? No one today, he said, speaks of orphans and orphanages, these terms are thankfully obsolete, but one can only suppose that a circumstance of this kind might account for the peculiarity of so untypical a boy. When I learned that at the Foundation the chief praisesong of their worship is cantillated in the language spoken by Our Lord, I invited him to have the run of my library, where he might find volumes of theological and historical appeal. He brightened at this, but only fleetingly. Unhappily his diffidence was such that he shrank from entering my study. Yet what Reverend Greenhill asked of me, Ned said, was impossible. To be seen in the company of a leper with a leper's name? I was myself too much the target of nasty cracks.

In Ned's tone, I should add, there was nothing of complaint or grievance. He spoke with simple matter-of-factness, whether improvised or not. And somehow I could not resist asking if he recalled that it was I who had dared to befriend Ben-Zion Elefantin: did he remember that? Oh, he said, passing your open door on my way for my hour with Reverend Greenhill, I once saw the two of you bent over some sort of board game, and of course like everyone else I knew the rowdies had you in their sights, as they had me, but I put it out of my mind. The truth is it gave me a twinge of guilt. I did badly that day with my Xenophon.

After this, I turned rather self-consciously away from this subject to a blander one, and when we shook hands and parted and I was back in my office, I requested one of the clerks to look up a certain Elijah Foundation and make a note of the results. In the end he found nothing; such an entity no longer exists, and why should it, after so many decades? And why is it plausible that Ned Greenhill's recollection of words uttered a lifetime ago to a vulnerable child of ten should hold water? And besides, is it not likely that it was a different boy Reverend Greenhill spoke of all those years before? And not Ben-Zion Elefantin?

But for the rest of that day I was unaccountably thrown into an unusual dejection, and if not for the kind concern of my own good Peg (Miss Margaret Stimmer as she was then), I might not have recovered my spirits. Nor have I since met with Ned Greenhill.

*

August 9, 1949. For the last several hours I have been ruminating over what I have come more and more to think of as Ben-Zion Elefantin's entreaty. How fragile it is, and yet how persuasive! My transcription, so called, of Ben-Zion Elefantin's history continues to occupy my father's cigar box, forbidden to any eye but my own. It will be plain to the excluded reader that here he will find himself at a disadvantage. And for good reason: my growing apprehension. Is Ben-Zion Elefantin's testimony, if I may take it to be that, a wizardly act of my own deceit? His pleadings are the very marrow, and may I say the soul, of my memoir, and when I lift them out of their shelter (as I must shamelessly admit I am too often tempted to do) I am made heartsick, as by the hovering of a revenant. And sometimes, in these sluggish midafternoons when I am seized by an overpowering stupor, I seem to see my father's cigar box elide into the pretty china dish where my mother kept the scarab ring she never wore.

*

August 13, 1949. Hideous. Horrible and hideous. I cannot cleanse my eyes of it. Hedda's shriek, and then Amelia running through the corridors shouting for me to come, come, come! That thing, barely a man, dangling in the night from

the lit chandelier with its head horribly loos-
ened, the tongue bulging, the necktie and its yel-
low butterflies twisted tight around the throat,
the glass beads and teardrops swaying and tinkling like harps

*

August 14, 1949. At three o'clock this afternoon,
mindful of the time gap, I telephoned my son.
Noon in Los Angeles. He was still asleep, I could
not help myself, I have no one dear to me, how
alone I am, I feel strangled by my own vagrant
fears. I despised this man, I thought him infantile in his attachment, the close companion of a
vandal, if not himself a vandal, the two of them
a cabal of criminality. But to take his own life
because he could not bear the grieving, what
am I to make of this? My son is indifferent to all
of it, the suicide of a stranger, but what of my
own hurt, how can he not see it, the fickleness
of life, the cryptic trail of the past (my father's
desertion of my mother), and what of his own

futility? I often feel that my son grudges me his time, yet today he took me by surprise, showing no impatience, assuring me there was no intrusion and that anyhow he had lately been sleeping lightly, buoyed up by what was almost certain to become his breakthrough, and do I know who William Wyler is? Wyler himself, he said, not his assistant, promises to get to my treatment early next week, likes the basic idea, seems excited by it, and so forth and so on, and how many times have I been apprised of this mirage by my deluded son? The oasis is always over the next hill. And the next hill is always more of the same desert.

I am not a jealous man. As a person of lineage, and as the heir and partner of a highly reputable law firm, I have never had a reason to envy. Rather, throughout my career, others have envied me. My father, had he lived to know of it, would have been pleased by at least the outward course of my life, my early achievements (e.g., editor in chief, Yale Law Journal), my marriage into a family similar in standing to our own, and whatever considerable esteem I have earned in the civic area. Despite the recklessness of his youth, my father was for the entirety of his remaining days a wholly conventional man, with conventional expectations. I believe I have met them. That my son has not met mine is a lasting and festering bruise. Every month or so I read of yet another landmark acquisition by Edwin Jacobs Greenhill, Jr., the most recent being the Algonquin, a hotel famous thirty years ago for its literary cachet, and by my count his fourth such midtown purchase.

Ned, I am aware, has grandchildren. My son is two years older than Ned's. Both are middle-aged men. Can a treatment, so called, be said to possess literary cachet?

And I cannot, cannot, cannot cleanse my eyes of that horrific hanging thing.

*

August 19, 1949. Hedda has come to me with a substantial bundle of clothing, all of finest quality, just look here the linings and here also the stitches, and so many rich ties, this poor sickinthehead Mann dünn wie eine Krähe im Winter, she is sending these nice things to a charity, would I like to keep two or three of the neckties?

I told her I would not.

In describing my father as conventional some days ago, I meant it as a praiseworthy trait, perhaps as much for myself as for him. But nothing of that can be true. My God, how I falsify! There were certain times in my childhood, well before I was sent to the Academy, and when my mother was preoccupied elsewhere (she often spent evenings at one or another event at her Women's Club), I would see my father settle into a chair in his study with his newspaper, and angrily toss it away, and sit and stare at the glass door of the cabinet that held his collection. For long minutes he would open that door and stare, or he would stare through the glass with the door shut. He never took out any of these objects. I was always a little afraid of him during these motionless scenes, when he seemed as wooden and lifeless as one of my toy soldiers. I would be crouched on the carpet nearby watching for his breath to resume, hoping my mother would come home and this silent and wooden starer would turn back into the father I knew.

It is because of these distant impressions that now and then assault me in unheralded snatches of panic that I believe my father harbored somewhere in his ribs an untamed creature. Unlike him, I am no dissembler, I am subject to no fantastic imaginings. And yet I feel all at sea, my memoir is of no more import than some wild pestilential growth, and what idiocy it was to think that it could be chained, as originally proposed, by ten typewritten sheets!

*

September 2, 1949. 4 PM. It is now nearly two weeks since with some urgency I advised Mr. John Theory, my current liaison at Morgan, of the need for the transfer of one of the Trustees here to a nursing facility. This morning there came from him what I expected to be confirmation, however delayed, of the completed arrangements, while meanwhile the disrepute brought upon this house by the disgrace of suicide has erased all such necessity; so it may be that what is merely moot is finally the father of the ironical. I have since learned that John's communication, disturbing in the extreme, has been received by all five remaining Trustees. We are informed that the present situation at Temple House has long been unsustainable, that after private surveillance by the bank it was determined that the physical and financial condition of the premises continues to deteriorate (vermin, easy access by intruders, insufficient outdoors safety for the residents, understaffing, fragile old books a flammable hazard in the kitchen area, etc.), that the ill-considered renovations of so many years ago are inappropriate for the residents (dangerously weighty ceiling lighting fixtures, the attractive nuisance of a dimly lit chapel no longer in use), and so forth. In brief: we are required to vacate Temple House by no later than December 15, 1949.

By this hour (7:30 PM) the letters have been read in, it must be said, a flurry of consternation. My colleagues, uninvited, invaded my study shortly after the lunch trays were removed (Hedda has not yet been told of this new calamity), chiefly to bemoan the disruption, as if I, because of my prior interaction with John Theory, were the cause of it. Once again I find I am accused, not surprisingly by one of my earlier accusers, the nonentity who came together with that pernicious twosome to charge me with disturbing the peace. I will not forget that ignominious hammer and tongs, his sole utterance, nor will I give his name. Let him and the others be expunged from my consciousness.

Note how consistent I have been in omitting all names but that of Ned Greenhill, of whom I suspect no ill intent. (For obvious reasons, he

was never regarded as eligible to serve as Trustee,
yet to this day he has never shown resentment
or rancor.) My honorable colleagues, it goes
without saying, spare no opportunity to deni-
grate me. I blame this on that insidious Amelia,
who coming one evening to pick up my dinner
tray (once again that vile stew), observed me in
an idle moment of contemplation. Randomly
dispersed on my table, close to my father's cigar
box (with its hidden burden), were a few of his
cherished arcana. I say randomly; I should perhaps say dreamily, as when some unforgotten
presence presses as palpably as if it were as near
and true as living pulse. It seemed to me that I
was again on the floor with my wooden brigade,
my father was again staring through the glass
door, while meanwhile in the cup of my hand
lay the bulbous female contours of one of those
grotesque figurines, no more than three inches in
height, that are prominent among his findings.
And here was Amelia spewing out her lascivious
giggle and going off, as I soon understood, to

spread an infamous aspersion: that I am in the grip of an obscene habit of some kind. Since then, I have been subject to muted but sly hints and taunts, implying that I am given to caress the stone breasts and vulvae of these innocent objects. My worthy peers, elderly widowers all, display the spiteful conduct of a pack of kindergartners!

Hedda herself often remarks on these juvenile provocations in similar vein, having, as she recently confided, until 1932 taught at Vienna's most respected fortschrittliche Grundschule. I think of her as a mundane intelligence, and never presumed she could be formally equipped with what she calls a Masterstudium. And with her dark looks she is certainly not a native Austrian. I have so far had little interest in her bizarre wanderings, though it bemuses me to learn that she was obliged to spend years in some woebegone Caribbean village, where, she insists, the thuggish Trujillo was more open to persons like herself than the American president. (Miranda and

I, to tell the truth, naturally cast our votes four times against Roosevelt's socialist schemes, even as we were compelled to overcome our dislike of that near-socialist Wendell Willkie.)

But already today the plans for decampment have begun. The Trustees, to say it outright, are wealthy men: relocation ought not to be a difficulty. But where is one to go?

*

September 3, 1949. When this morning I was finally able to reach John Theory (he is rarely at his desk), he replied with a disconcerting testiness, though his telephone manner has in the past never been anything but respectful. Three generations of Petries, I told him, have been with Morgan, and out of the blue you have the gall to put me out on the street? Now listen to me, Lloyd, he said, there is nothing sudden or abrupt here, three months ago I sent you, I mean you personally as designated spokesman for the residents of Temple House, to which position you will recall you readily agreed some four years ago, an official notice stating that an investigation of the condition of the property was soon to begin. You cannot claim, he said, to be surprised. I am acutely surprised, I said, and as for the safety of our environment here, ought that not to be the Trustees' own consideration without extraneous intrusion? Read the Charter, Lloyd, he said (with a good deal of asperity), why don't you just read the Charter, and in fact I returned to it some twenty minutes ago and to my embarrassment located the clause in question. On its face it appears to contradict the earlier in-perpetuity clause, but on further examination I see that some clever Shylock's statutory legerde-main obviates this conflict.

More to the point, I have also found the letter of prior notification John speaks of. It troubles me that I had entirely forgotten it. I believe it must be my immersion in my memoir at the time of its arrival that distracted me, but what is still more vexing is that I discovered this letter in my father's cigar box interleaved among the transcription papers, and have no memory of inserting it there. What could I have been thinking, or was I thinking at all? I have never been subject to carelessness, and surely not to willful negligence. Nevertheless it does not escape me that this new crop of rash young bankers is wanting in both decorum and deference.

★

September 5, 1949. Labor Day. Apparently hoping to compensate for Amelia's recent barbarism, Hedda has come with a page torn out from Life magazine: a large photo of Sigmund Freud's desk in his Vienna study. Parading over its surface are innumerable antiquities similar to my father's, though certainly surpassing his in quantity. See now, Hedda said, one of the greatest thinkers of the century, and no one dares to accuse such a man of Lüsternheit! Clearly she means to flatter (or is it comfort?) me, as if I ought to be impressed by a comparison with this charlatan Jew and his preposterous notions. It can easily be seen throughout my memoir that I have no regard for such absurd posturings; it is the conscious mind I value, not its allegedly secret underworld. So here is this ragged bit of paper (she leaves it on my table and runs off), with all these phantasmagoric pharaonic remnants, bellies and horns, faceless heads, and why do these unfathomable things lead me to remember the heat of Ben-Zion Elefantin's bony shins against my own?

*

September 18, 1949. An unexpected public affliction, this buzzing and swarming of sons and sons-in-law and daughters and daughters-in-law and grandsons and granddaughters, and who knows whatever other likely kin never before known to have been seen on these premises, soon to be razed and replaced by what faddish excrescence? I continue to follow in the Times how that predatory clique of New York developers are sniffing opportunities here in Westchester, with Temple House and its considerable grounds as prime prey. Undoubtedly the maples will give way to asphalt, though today they are all gold, gold at their crowns, gold on the paths, gold gilding the old benches. Our last fall here. The fall of Temple House. And the visitors, the half-forgotten relations, the would-be heirs and successors, coming, as they say, to the rescue, the plans for departure, the summonings, the offerings, the temptings, the resolutions, the invitations, the reassurances: this unwonted outbreak of the fevers of hospitality. Old men's bones will be ash before long; inconceivable that wealthy old men should languish unhoused.

As for me, with no eruption of daughter-in-law or grandchild or so much as a willing cousin (the latter-day Petries and Wilkinsons have hardly been fruitful), yet I too have a son, have I not?

Some days ago I informed him of our enforced exodus. He did not beseech me to fly at once to Los Angeles for a new life in the California sunshine. Oh Dad, he said, you know you wouldn't fit in here, it's not your milieu, you wouldn't be happy, and anyhow it's not a generational thing, it's a personality difference: and more demurrals on the same theme. He claims to be studying a freeing philosophy, Oriental in origin, called Zen, as well as the writings of one Martin Buber. (All this astonished me. I am alarmed by these inconstant dilettantisms.) I explained that to lighten the burden of my imminent move, I am about to dispose of much of my material possessions, as well as of certain keepsakes, one of which he had at one time expressed a strong desire to get hold of. I regret my untoward obstinacy in refusing you, I told him, and would be glad to assist in whatever motion picture project you are currently engaged in. I speak not only of financing, though we can surely discuss such an eventuality. Are you, I asked, still interested in making some use of my father's notes on his Egyptian travels, and his inscrutable desertion of my mother, and his unusual friendship with Sir Flinders Petrie? Oh no Dad, he said, it's past time for that sort of thing, not another one of these Near Eastern Westerns with the weeping abandoned bride, thanks all the same. And he made no further mention of William Wyler.

There is no way I can win back my son: not by bribery, not by appeasement. Not by a love I cannot feel. I have loved only twice. Once my glorious Peg. And once, long ago, Ben-Zion Elefantin.

*

September 22, 1949. How many hours we lay there entwined I cannot say, nor can I recall whether either of us had surrendered, as I now suppose, to what must have been a kind of half-sleep. For myself, I know that the sun crept from one corner of the ceiling to another, and that I tracked its slow progress with indolent eyes. Nor can I say that I was fully awake, though the murmurings that swirled around me were remnants of Ben-Zion Elefantin's small low catlike growlings, rising and ebbing, so that here and there I took him to be invoking a foreign tongue, even as I apprehended his meaning. By now the far-off football shouts had diminished, and a commotion in the corridors signaled that the dinner hour had arrived, and that our classmates had begun their raucous rush to the refectory. This reminded me that I was parched; my palate was no better than a dry ribbed plain, and while Ben-Zion Elefantin, with his curious patience, peeled away the shell of his boiled egg, I drank innumerable cups of water, as if my thirst could consume some bottomless Niagara. I had no hunger at all. We sat, he and I, in a quiet made more dense by the clamor all around, and said nothing, until he pushed his chair back from the table and left me. This time I did not follow.

If only lost minutes could be reconstructed

(minutes, I mean, in a boy's mind seventy years ago), I would today perhaps understand what I understood only faintly then. He was throwing me off, he had no wish for me to pursue him. Something there was in me that had made him ashamed. It was my pity he felt; he recoiled from it. Pity, he knew, was no more than blatant disbelief. Or else it was belief: that I thought him crazed. It may be that I did think him crazed, as a fabricator is crazed by the dazzle of his fabrication. And indeed I was dazzled, as I am even now, by the ingenuity of his fable, if that is what it was, and by the labyrinth of his boyish brain. And by the piteous loneliness of his thin legs. He had abandoned me once before, when I had misunderstood his words; but his words were like no other boy's words, so how was I to blame? And am I not myself the son of a crazed father, so how am I to blame?

The reader will conclude that I am mistaking pity for love.

Conclude however you please.

And for a second time (this was in chapel the next morning, when Reverend Greenhill's text was Jonah's refusal to preach to Nineveh), I saw yet again how humbly Ben-Zion Elefantin could sink into his shoulder blades as if to hide from himself. I am sorry, he said, that I made you so thirsty. You didn't make me thirsty, I said, I just was. But I did make you thirsty, he said. Look, I said, come to my room at recess, there's something I want to show you. I never want anyone else to see it, you're the only one. All right, he said, I will come. Or maybe, I said, I'll bring it to your room because you always keep your door shut. And then Reverend Greenhill began to describe the big fish, which he explained wasn't necessarily an actual whale, and to my surprise I found myself listening with some interest.

*

September 24, 1949. It was on this day seven years ago that my poor Peg passed on. I have visited her burial site only on three particular occasions (I think of these as our small private anniversaries), and never since the last. Like me, she had no siblings, and her parents were long gone, so it was I who arranged for her spare marble gravestone in St. Mark's Episcopal Cemetery, a short drive not far from Temple House. (Her origins were midwest Methodist, but no matter.) I had intended to go there often, to reflect on the words I had myself composed: Margaret Gertrude Stimmer, A Companion Valorous and Pure. I had hoped that this would give me if not consolation, then the will to bear her absence; yet before long I learned to my chagrin that my repeated presence there provoked unpleasant gossip among my colleagues. (My own interment, as is fitting, will be beside Miranda in the Petrie family plot.)

*

September 25, 1949. Once again the anxieties of my present musings disrupt my focus and send my thoughts flying: what am I to do with my father's things, where am I to go, and will I be compelled to jettison my Remington? Even so, these insecurities must not sway me from the urgency of my purpose. Then let it be noted that in the very hour of my assignation with Ben-Zion Elefantin, recess was suspended. Instead, Forms Four through Eight were required to attend a lecture, to be held in the refectory, by a respected acquaintance of Reverend Greenhill's, whose name has disappeared from my memory, though I can still see his thin pale fingers fluttering over the buttons of his vest as if in a failing plea for our unruly attention. Gentlemen, Reverend Greenhill began (he addressed us thus in the aggregate, though otherwise he called each boy by his family name), our subject today, however geographically distant, transpires, so to say, before our very eyes, while the fires of injustice are rank in our nostrils. Our speaker, he went on, is a formidable scholar of this shameful period in the history of France. Listen carefully, because it contains lessons for us at this very moment, here in our noble Temple Academy. It is a tale of lie and libel and deceit, and there is much to glean from it even for such a privileged society as ours. The visitor, it turned out, was too short for the height of the lectern; it rose to the bottom of his chin, so that his head seemed to hover on its own, bodiless. Captain Dreyfus, he said, is an officer in the French military who in a public ceremony of deliberate humiliation has been wrongfully stripped of his epaulets, but here he was interrupted: what are epaulets, sir, are they something like underpants? Against barbs such as this the little man struggled on in what soon became an assault of chatter and titter, as by twosomes and threesomes his audience dwindled. And when I furtively gestured to Ben-Zion Elefantin to come away, he glared at me with a ferocity I did not recognize, and remained where he was.

For days afterward the rowdies made much of this event in their harryings, with taunts of you are rank in my nostril and other such inspired vituperations, stripped epaulets not least among them. And in chapel on Sunday Reverend Greenhill announced that he intended to take a week's holiday in the Hebrides, to follow, he said, in the footsteps of Boswell and Dr. Johnson.

*

September 28, 1949. The exodus is under way. Two have already departed, one to Florida (the hammer-and-tongs fellow, and good riddance), the other ostensibly to vacation in Switzerland, where his nephew has business connections as well as a pied-à-terre in Zurich. I take vacation to be a euphemism for the final adieu: this chap, a veteran of kidney stones, can barely pump out three words without losing his breath, and who knows how he will survive a plane trip of many hours? Next week, I hear, two more of our sorry cohort are to vanish, the first to what is nowadays known as a senior residence, the second to a furnished annex, formerly a garage, directly behind his sister-in-law's home in nearby Bronxville. (His brother is deceased.) As I earlier remarked, the Trustees are far, far from being pinched for dollars, and were never likely to be dependents, yet what else is longevity if not dependency?

We were seven, and then six, and then five, and now with the exit of four, there remains but one, and I am that one. Not that I am entirely alone. Amelia, seeing the imminent collapse of her engagement here, has gone off to Texas with her newest casanova (so says Hedda), but Hedda herself persists. I go down to the kitchen for meals; it simplifies, or else call it democratization. We sit side by side and sometimes together pull out from their shelves in the pantry two or three of Reverend Greenhill's disorderly mélange of old books, unwanted everywhere, though Hedda thinks this inconceivable. Why not take whatever you please, I tell her, they will anyhow end in the dumpster along with the much abused chapel pews. Danke, aber nein,

only this one I take, and showed me the title,
Liederkreis von Heinrich Heine.

★

September 30, 1949. I had determined to carry
what I knew to be my father's foremost treasure to Ben-Zion Elefantin's room, relying on
his obstinately shut door to ensure our privacy.
But I hung back: it was there, amid the float-
ing dust particles, that we had lain leg over leg,
as if trapped together in the soft maze of some
spider's web, and under the shawl of a solitude
and gravity that frightened me. My instinct
was to keep away, and my own room, exposed
to any passerby (I was too cowardly to flout the
rules), was anyhow unsuitable for my devising.
My devising was, as I dimly felt it, a consecra-
tion of sorts. The chapel was bare of such sensa-
tions, and besides, we had once been discovered
there. Then what of Reverend Greenhill's sanc-
tum? No one entered unless summoned, not

even the masters, though according to his own dictum, Reverend Greenhill's study door was never closed, either by his wish or by any key. Gentlemen, he once told us (his text that day was the serpent in Eden), I own nothing of value but my library and my reflections; my books are mere matter, my reflections are not. It was off-putting to think (no doubt a derisive invention of the rowdies) that he kept on his table a photograph of his dead wife, or was it his dead child, with a wilting lily before it. But no pupil who was called to stand at that table had ever reported seeing anything like this. It was the carpet that surprised, a meadowlike flourish of purple flowers and curled fronds; it appeared to be Reverend Greenhill's sole indulgence. We who remembered Mr. Canterbury's introduction of this luxury knew better. And anyhow Reverend Greenhill had requested before his departure that every middle- and upper-form boy study his Geography of Great Britain and put a green mark, if he could find them, on the Hebrides.

As for the carpet: I have since come to believe that monastic zeal conceals a sybarite.

★

October 4, 1949. It was on this carpet that we settled in our customary chess posture, I uneasily on one side, he on the other, with my shoebox between us. I had fixed the hour at eleven that night, when both masters and boys were safely asleep, while in some distant valley Reverend Greenhill, as I supposed, was stalking the spoor of those venerated names I had already forgotten. I am sorry, Ben-Zion Elefantin said, that I declined to come away when you asked. That stupid lecture, what a bore, I said, why would you want to stay? Oh, he said, this man they shamed, he is loyal and they say he is disloyal, it is as if he is Elefantin, but you are my friend and once more I have disappointed you. You haven't, it's just the way you are, I said, and got up to pull aside the curtains at the big paneled windows to let in the light. It was no more than pale misty moonlight, but it was enough; it wouldn't do to switch on the lamp on Reverend Greenhill's table. Even as late as it was, some lone boy on his way to the toilet might see the brightness under the doorsill and spy on us. Look, I said, I've brought you something important. It's only for you, no one else would understand.

And again I told him that my father had once traveled to Egypt, and while sailing upstream on the Nile had observed on his left the jumbled greenery of Elephantine Island and the white masses of storks crowding the banks. I told him more: I said that my father, fresh from Sir Flinders Petrie's tutelage, had recognized from afar the broken earth mounds of abandoned excavations, and had ordered his guide to take him ashore. No, the guide said, there has come recently a very strong khamsin, it tears up the ground and overturns the ruins, it is not safe now to tread there. But my father insisted, and the two of them picked their way through silted

stones and newborn chasms while the guide
went on groaning his refusal. It was here, pulled
up from a deep ditch resembling a tunnel, that
my father found what I keep in this box.

The reader may well wonder at these prevarications. Nothing of the sort is recorded in
my father's fading notes as I have described them
here. Under the woolen socks that covered my
shoebox I had hidden what I felt to be a tribute, a
token, a proof, though of what? For a long time I
was unknowing; but now nothing was obscured
and I knew and I knew and I knew. Our knees,
our shoulders, our breathings, had touched. It
was as if the crisis of my father's desires were
destined to fall upon such a bony specter as Ben-
Zion Elefantin; yet I was in fear of his repug-
nance, and of my own diffidence before it. I had
seen how the meek bent of his scrawny shoulders could flame into an obdurate certainty:
would he scoff at my father's chief finding as he
had scoffed at all the others? And how could he
dare to scoff if I convinced him, however falsely,

of my father's credibility? And of the khamsin and the silted stones and the storks?

Then I took out from my shoebox the beaker with its long stork's neck and its one emerald eye.

Here it is, I said, it's for you, I want you to have it. You can show it to your parents to decide if it's real. It can't be fake, my father didn't get it from some shady shopkeeper or anything fishy like that. Look, it's in the shape of a stork! No, he said, not a stork, the body of the ibis is white like a stork's but the beak is black and curved downward. All right, I said, but it's yours anyway, it was meant for you, some day you will be going from here, your parents will send for you. Oh, he said, I can never predict when my uncle will come, and my parents are far away.

I felt his reluctance. I saw that he preferred silence, turning his hungry face to the silhouetted shelves of Reverend Greenhill's books, as if by his look he could swallow them all. The carpet under the deluding moonlight seemed all at once botanically alive, a real garden, with rose-red petals and grass-green stalks, and the beaker standing on its base of avian knees like some wild wayward bird that had lost its way and landed there. The minutes of quiet took on the gravity of the ceremonial, though I could not have named it that, nor am I confident even now of that sacerdotal term. What I knew was only that something crucial, some merciless thirst, was at stake: that my connection, however fearful or tenuous, with Ben-Zion Elefantin must not be cut off. Sooner or later he would leave. Sooner or later I would never see him again. He put out his hand to me and I took it. Thank you, he said, but it is impossible, what is such a vessel to me?

He left me behind then, as one would abandon a person infected by plague. I somehow understood, for a reason I cannot unravel, that this was not the first time he had come to this place in the night.

*

October 7, 1949. My evenings with Hedda in the kitchen are quite pleasant. Only yesterday she confided that she has begun to look for employment elsewhere, but is willing to stay on until I know where I am to go. To my relief, she has agreed to substitute lighter fare for those dense stews, and my digestion is much the better for it. In addition, we have fallen into a practice entirely alien to my experience. I was at first acutely embarrassed. Her idea struck me as a foolish game, and under normal circumstances I believe it would surely be so. She had removed from the pantry shelves (at my urging, it may be recalled) the work of some foreign poet, and not long ago showed me, on facing pages, an English version. She would read aloud from the German, she proposed, and I was to do the same for the translation. I dislike the sounds of that distasteful language, but when I see how at home she is in those growly syllables, and how they transform her from an inconsequential domestic to a woman who thinks, I am, I admit, carried

away. I can still remember verbatim all four lines
of the verse that uncannily fell to me:

At first I almost despaired,
And thought I would never be able to bear it;
Yet even so, I have borne it—
But do not ask me how.

My lost and dearest Peg, Valorous and Pure.
It is as if this long-dead Jew (so Hedda tells me
he is), of whom I know nothing, mourns in my
own voice.

And here, in the helter-skelter of Reverend Greenhill's books, many with their leaves
gnarled by the steam of kettles and stewpots over
the years, you have only to put in your hand and
pull out a plum: my son's current idée fixe, so to
say, unless he has already fled off to other fanta-
sies. I and Thou, a little thing, no thicker than a
pamphlet, by this Buber he spoke of. Yet another
Jew. I have looked into it: impenetrable.

Hedda's anxious perusal of the help-wanted

columns puts me in mind of a public resource I have never before contemplated using. My immediate intention is to place brief advertisements in various newspapers, not excluding the tabloids, in the hope of relieving me of the dread that too often worries my nights. If this small scheme should reveal nothing, well and good. And if a reply should come, what am I to think?

*

October 12, 1949. This morning an extraordinary telephone call from Ned Greenhill. I regret being out of touch, he said, how long has it been since that fine afternoon at the Oyster Bar? I hear they are tearing the place apart and redoing it from scratch, dozens of new hires and so forth, it seems the world doesn't stand still. And how are you in general, Lloyd? Comfortably suspended in lassitude, I told him; but I dislike these obligatory maunderings that conceal an as yet unspoken purpose. Oh yes, he said, everything up in the air, what's to become of the old mausoleum in the woods? That thicket of antediluvian maples always gave me a feeling, especially at night, of wolves prowling there, it wouldn't be a loss to have them come down, roots and all. The real estate section in last week's Tribune, if you happened to see it, was full of probable buyers. Yes, I said, I saw that, and isn't your son one of them? Well Lloyd, he said, it's problematic, the place has a history, not altogether unsavory, and typical of its era after all, so there's some vestige of nostalgia, don't you think, at least for the likes of us elderly fellows. I've told Edwin, keep it low, don't go too high, but this new generation's got no use for such ideas, it's nothing but taller and taller, so how would you feel, Lloyd, about relocating to the fifteenth floor over on East Seventy-sixth? Used to be the old Winthrop Court, Edwin's converting it into a live-in hotel, all the amenities, maid service and so on. And an actual courtyard, a little private garden of shrubs and paths, all hidden from any casual pedestrian eye. Very fine restaurants in the vicinity, as I can personally testify. I know you've all had to get out of that moth-eaten wreck, I heard this only last week from John Theory, turns out he's a classmate of Edwin's at Amherst. It would do you good to get away from the grasshoppers and back into the life of the city, so what do you say? And understand me, Lloyd, except for taxes and suchlike this would be something I hope you'd accept as a tribute from me.

Our conversation went on for more than two hours. He explained that his son planned for the initial tenants to be of a certain standing, in order to lure others of similar status. A prestige building, they call it. And because of our old connection, Ned said, for you, Lloyd, and solely for you, the fifteenth-floor suite has been set aside, if you would accept it, as a lifetime gift from me, though who knows which of us will go graveward first. So Lloyd, he said, you'll think about it, won't you?

Of course I pressed him to tell what could

possibly have motivated this inconceivable gesture. His response was at bottom offensive, and on three counts. First, I am a man of dignified wealth in my own right, not to be regarded as a recipient of another man's benefaction. Second, wittingly or not, he flaunts his son's prosperity when he is fully aware of my own paternal disappointment. Third, lurking below this seeming generosity of heart, is its price: I am to serve as a decoy to further his son's ambition. I had thought better of Ned, but much like his portion of the bulk of mankind, he puts his own interest first, undeniably sugar-coated by reminiscence.

Of his recollections, and his claims, I recognize very little. I knew him from a distance; I knew him hardly at all. In those hurtful years at the Academy, he told me, there were only two persons who regarded him with decency. One was Reverend Greenhill and the other was Lloyd Petrie. You never put me down, Lloyd, you never called me Hebe, and that time when a mob of them came and tore whole pages out of my

Greek grammar, you had nothing to do with it.
You were among the very few who kept away. I
was suffering all those years at school, Lloyd, and
it's not something a person forgets. You never
went out of your way to do me harm.

I was embarrassed by all this untempered
emotion. That is how these people are, their
overflowing sentimentalism. Their motion picture style of exaggerated feeling. Well, I said, I
do remember that awful night, they had ciga-
rettes and burned holes in your sheets. But why,
I asked, did you think I would do any of that sort
of thing? Because, he said, you were a Petrie.
You were one of them, you thought it was your
right.

This, I must acknowledge, unsettled me. I
was a Petrie then, and I am a Petrie now. It is for
this very reason that Ned, through his son, offers
me an advantage, is it not? I could not tell him,
if he failed to discern it for himself, that I had
been deprived of my right, as he put it, because
I had been contaminated by Ben-Zion Elefantin.

I dared not tell him how fervently I had longed to be reinstated.

Instead, I firmly declined his largesse.

It is true that I never called him Hebe; but I thought it. And sometimes, I admonish myself, I still think it.

*

October 18, 1949. There has not been a single reply to my numerous advertisements, though with some trepidation at how outlandish it was, I went so far as to place one in the Jewish Day, a local journal whose existence I have only just now come upon. I kept my anonymity, of course, and supplied only a postal box number. My language too was sparse and direct: if you, I wrote, were at any time ever associated with a children's home known as the Elijah Foundation, please respond. A far-fetched effort. Boys of twelve seventy years ago would likely today be dead men. I am happy not to have uncovered

Ben-Zion Elefantin by this means, or anyone who knew him. And better yet, it promises that he was never a boy sent over to the Academy by some shabby almshouse that has not survived. Absence itself is a kind of proof.

*

October 20, 1949. It is by now several days since that abrasive talk with Ned Greenhill. On second thought, I believe I will accept his invitation, but on a gentleman's terms and decidedly sans his benevolence. I am a practical man, as I often say, and the hard truth is that I have nowhere else to lay my head.

As for his son: if these forlorn precincts should fall into his hands, how high will he go?

*

November 3, 1949. For the remainder of that school term I saw far too little of Ben-Zion Elefantin.

Something poisonous had come between us: a remoteness beyond my understanding. When he gave me his hand that fevered winter night on the flowered carpet, it was hot and moist, as if he had combed it through dew. I had no inkling that I would never again know the slightness of his palm or the frailty of his small knuckles. And once more his door was shut against me, and again I would catch the bleats and driftings of what passed for liturgical grumbles, or else the muted wail of some secret weeping; but he was two years older than I, and thereby too old to cry. I, alone on my bed with my disordered chessboard before me, was not.

In the refectory he sat at a distance, and I saw that he spoke to no one, and no one spoke to him. But at certain unaware moments I would feel his look. It was, I thought, altogether washed clean of the meek and the humble. In chapel too he kept apart, and was intent, as always, on the sermon, though of late Reverend Greenhill's homiletics had departed from the biblical, and for several Sundays in a row he chose as his theme his recent adventures in the Hebrides. His holiday there, he said, had been inspired by Samuel Johnson, a famous Englishman of virtue and wisdom who lived two hundred years ago; and also by James Boswell, a Scotsman equally famous and virtuous. The loyalty to each other of these two friends, he told us, was such that Boswell gave his life to recording the life of Johnson, particularly during a journey to the Hebrides the two of them together undertook.

It was clear that he meant us to seize the meaning of this lesson: friendship and loyalty and attentiveness and decorum. (To illustrate the latter, he read out a paragraph of Boswell's prose.) All this, I saw, was aimed at the rowdies; but they kept their heads down and were quiet. Or else were drawn in by his tale of crags and abysses, and of ships broken on rocks in the waters that skirt the islands, and especially of a frightening fall from a mossy cliff. (Here, in a sort of purposeful drama, Reverend Greenhill held up his elbow, fractured and healing, he said, but painful still.) And I thought: I have been loyal to Ben-Zion Elefantin, how unfair that he is disloyal to me.

Today as I write (in one of these formless fits of longing and loss that sometimes flood me), it occurs to me to ask: in the many pages of my memoir that heap up under my hand, am I not Ben-Zion Elefantin's Boswell? It discomfits me to think that if I am Boswell, the small figure I was once so achingly devoted to imagined himself to be Dreyfus.

*

November 12, 1949. I have spoken before of those wretched showers of our youth: a common space of two overhead nozzles, heated by a coal stove that spat out its fickle warmth no more than inches from its maw. Two showerheads to serve one hundred pupils, with five minutes allotted for each, no matter the season; but from

November to March the queue was not long. A boy would prefer to stink, and many did, rather than endure the frigid air of this glacial hell, or the water that was colder than air. It was here that I found myself unexpectedly alone with Ben-Zion Elefantin. He stood before me wet and naked and shivering, and I the same before him; but the blaze of his hair was darkened by water, and his ribs were as skeletal as his pitiful knees. His bare feet were paler than his hands. Without his cap and his blazer, he seemed smaller than ever. Nearly a month had gone by with not a syllable between us. I felt a little afraid; what must I say?

I asked him why.

He said nothing. So again I asked why.

Because I believed you were my friend.

I *am* your friend, I said.

And again he said nothing. You have to tell me why, I said, you have to.

A cloud of vapor spilled out of his mouth, and I saw the same rise up from mine. It was hard to breathe in that place.

But it's real. You saw for yourself that it's real. And your parents, you told me they buy and sell such things.

They keep me safe from them. That is why I am sent to school. To keep me from abomination.

I knew this word. Mr. Canterbury had spoken it in chapel many times.

And it was Ben-Zion Elefantin's last word to me. I can hear it now, in a kind of self-willed hallucination: that curiously wavering uncharted bookish voice of his own making. An orphaned voice of no known origin.

*

December 12, 1949. No uncle came for him. He remained with the Fourth Form, moved up to the Fifth and the Sixth and the Seventh, and I, in the Eighth, later that year, in June, wore cap and gown for Commencement. The ceremony was held in a capacious tent on the football field, equipped with row upon row of folding chairs to accommodate the mass of parents and well-wishers who were expected to attend. Or were, perhaps, not entirely expected, which may have explained why Reverend Greenhill had appointed the Seventh Form to fill most of the empty places, should there be any. At one side was the dais on which the graduates were to congregate, and at the other a long table freighted with lemonade and cinnamon ices and strawberries and scones heavily blanketed by chocolate syrup and caramel cream, the last an innovation of Reverend Greenhill's. (I heard him remark to one of the visitors that this violation of a traditional Scottish biscuit might not appeal to a fastidious palate, but the graduates were, after all, still boys.) As the procession shuffled forward to the blare of some hidden operatic loudspeaker, one could see a scattering of fathers, and with them the young women who from their age and attire, I now speculate, might be second wives, or even former nannies. The mothers, with their uplifted faces, were seated nearer the lectern, where Reverend Greenhill waited for the sounds of Aida to ebb. (My own mother was not among them. She had sent me a congratulatory note, fearing she would be too fatigued to sustain the long festivities.) First came the lesser prizes: for Attentiveness, for Patience, for Enterprise, for Courtesy, for Equestrian Skills, and all the rest; and then the Award for Excellence in Latin, renamed Classics (to include private study of Greek), won, predictably, by Edwin J. Greenhill. And following this, the Headmaster's Oration. Gentlemen, Reverend Greenhill began, I mean not to orate, but rather to bless. As you embark on this new phase of your lives, I hope you will carry with you the aspirations and virtues of our time-honored Academy, and that each of you will strive, as you grow into men, to be both a scholar and yes, a gentleman. But a scholar can be cruel, and a gentleman can be coarse. And here he read out, in his thin but reassuring voice, two passages from Scripture, the first from the Old Testament, the second from the New, in that order, he said, especially to note how the New and the Old are in harmony. A Jew named Abraham, he said, hastened to succor three parched strangers, and gave them water, and fed them, and cooled them from the sun in the shade of a tree, all unaware that they were angels. In the same way, we learn in the Gospel of Luke how a Samaritan, neither Jew nor Christian, found on the highway a man who had been beaten and robbed and lay nearly dead, and carried him to an inn and cared for him like a brother. And so, though I wish each graduate of our beloved Temple Academy for Boys to excel as a scholar and a gentleman, I hope that you will, above all, be kind.

Familiarity brought tedium. I half-heard all this, and at so distant a time I can barely give its gist. Besides, so commonplace in chapel were these exhortations, they might well have been tattooed on the palms of our hands. As for me, I had my eye on a brilliant red blemish at the edge of that restless puddle of Seventh Formers who had come to swell the assembly. Ben-Zion Elefantin was now fifteen, and nearly as small as before. I tried to catch his look, but his watchfulness seemed inward: on this day of farewell was he thinking of me, of how he cast me away for some preternatural cause? Was my father's stork, with its blinded eye, the abomination, or was it I?

Really, I ask myself to this very hour, was it I?

*

January 26, 1950. A catastrophe. How could this have happened? I blame it on my increasing forgetfulness, but how could I have forgotten what clings fast to my heart? Or perhaps I did not forget it, and those burly defectors Hedda called back from the city to pack up my things (one hundred or so boxes) carelessly left it behind? Too late now to retrieve it. Worse yet, given its weakened carriage and its increasing rust (that vinegar bath), was it mistaken for debris, and disposed of? The wrecking ball, I hear, has already had its way. So here I sit, with a bottle of ink before me, and my old Montblanc grudgingly resurrected (I had to replace the nib). In my eyrie on the highest floor of this solid old building the new windows admit no street noises, and the walls are inches thick. In this place no one could complain of my Remington! And I have nothing else as a sign of what was. Her grave is far away.

I am no longer accustomed to longhand, it tires my palsied wrists. (With my Remington it was the shoulders.) And even so fine a pen as a Montblanc can sometimes falter on a thin sheet of paper and spurt a droplet of ink; the cuff of my sleeve is spattered. No matter. I can see ahead almost to the close of my memoir; I am loath to put paid to it now. (I despise unfinished effort, as I have often reminded my son.) And then what will become of it? What of value or interest can it have? I have all along spoken of my reader, but can such a chimera exist? These days I sometimes feel as if I myself am a chimera: I walk the city streets in a cloud of uncertainty. I hardly know which way to turn, which is East and which is West. What was once second nature (the life of offices all around me, the lunches, the drinks, the handshake) dizzies me a little, the sidewalk density, the careless mob of unseeing people one must sidestep to avoid collision. Here and there the dirty pigeons, and overhead no birds. The absence of birds! The sky turned zigzag by the contours of this and that high-rise. And no trees.

It was my good fortune to have the December 15th date of eviction put off, though it inconvenienced the scheduled demolition and the difference affected the cost (which I was satisfied to reimburse). Ned Greenhill, or was it his son, managed to persuade Morgan (via John Theory) to allow me to remain through the holidays. Strange as it was, I spent Christmas Eve with Hedda in the kitchen. When Temple House was new, and the Trustees numbered twenty-five and the staff thirty-two, how convivial we were, all those fine fellows now long gone, the gossip, the overblown stories of old business triumphs, the somewhat modest tree (artificial, but genuine silver and costly), the feasting (stuffed goose and liver terrine and buttered shallots and curried lamb), and up and down the table, an infinite row of wines. And while I speak of remembered holidays, I am unhappy to mention that childhood's Christmases were more somber. The fir with its fragile colored glass globes and its gilt star nearly touching the ceiling, and the gaudily wrapped presents below, among them, I knew, the standard toy army and, one glorious year, my coveted chessmen. (Wooden, but I had dreamed of ivory.) And sometimes, when my mother seemed out of sorts and complained of feeling sick, it was only the two of us: my saddened father and I.

In our doomed and abandoned Temple House, Hedda had enlivened the kitchen as well as she could, hanging red and green crepe-paper streamers from cabinet door to cabinet door. The dinner, she told me, was to be anything I desired, but dessert must be a Viennese treat. I dreaded another Sacher torte; too much sugar makes my teeth ache. The pots on the stove were steaming as always, and while the oven was baking what-ever it might be, I was not unpleased to go on with our whimsical game. Hedda surprised me instead with what I supposed was a Christmas song (she had learned it in kindergarten, she said, and still remembered every word), as well as a scrap of paper in her own striving half-English. To me it has no holiday resonance of any kind, but I put it in my pocket and keep it still, if only to take note of Hedda's Teutonic script; and I record it here, I hardly know why.

A pine tree high in the North he lonely stands.
Under snow and wind he sleeps.
A palm tree he dreams a land to the East,
traurig on the desert sand.

If these words can claim some coherent sense, I cannot discern it; but when Hedda sang them in her emotional German, she appeared to feel its meaning. Her eyes were wet. North, East, what fleeings, what unwilled supplantings? The author, she reminded me, is the very one who echoed the loss of my darling Peg.

Yet the Christmases referenced above are, if I may say so, boilerplate. Certainly I favor tradition; I am aware that ancestral decorum ought not to be scorned. The aberrant is to be shunned. Life's fundamental rhythms depend on sameness, not deviation. All this I long ago learned from my mother.

Hedda's dessert turned out to be an elaborate pancake called (a name I cannot pronounce) Kaiserschmarren, filled with caramelized almonds and raisins soaked in rum. It did make my teeth ache; but the rum, she said, would numb the pain, and she brought out a sizable bottle and a cup for each of us, and poured a second cup, and a third, and at last a fourth, and then it was midnight. Enough there is yet also for New Year's, Hedda said, nicht wahr?

An anomaly. Out of the ordinary. A deviation from the natural. This homeless old man, this wandering Jewess.

*

January 27, 1950. These furnishings, these tables and chairs and credenzas and whatnot, make me uneasy. I suppose such modern geometries are the fashion in hotels that pretend to the comforts of luxury. Rectangular surfaces, ruler-straight legs, steel tops, nothing cushioned, nothing rounded. The bed, with its excessive pillows (they strain my back), has the width, or so it seems, of a horizonless continent. In the night, under a far-off ceiling, I see no end of vacuity. I feel myself a stranger in this bed, as I have not felt since my Academy cell: that narrow hard bed, my shoebox hidden beneath and my chessboard teetering on a bumpy blanket above. (And Ben-Zion Elefantin silently pondering.) Or not since the bed in which my son was conceived.

My Peg's sweet bed, there I was never a stranger.

★

January 29, 1950. Hedda telephones now and then (she is still unemployed), asking how I am, are my new surroundings pleasant, and so on; but as her world is scarcely akin to mine, I trust these exchanges will soon fade away.

★

February 2, 1950. The disadvantage of such a high floor is the beating of the wind on the panes. A disturbing noise, different from the tapping of rain. (There are times when the latter mimics the persistent diligence of my old Remington.) But a wild winter wind, especially at night, is frightening, like some misunderstood warning.

★

February 4, 1950. The reader, if he has not already abandoned me, will be reminded that he has been deliberately banned from viewing the contents of my father's cigar box. During the confusion and may I say the distress of my relocation, I myself rarely looked into it, but even now, while I have the leisure to parse its perplexities (and a lone nightly meal in a reputed restaurant turns out to be less appealing than the kitchen in Temple House), I am unable to fathom its origin or its mode. For want of something more plausible, I have on occasion described these papers as a transcription. And again as a plea. And again as a deposition. But for all their particularity, there is nothing verbatim here, and how could there be? I remember nothing. I remember everything. I believe everything. I believe nothing. The frenzied murmurings of two agitated boys prone and under a spell. A liar's screed, an invention? An apparition's fevered pedantry? And who knows such things, this garble of history and foreign babble? Not I. Nor am I a man of imagination.

Still, I must decide. Destroy what cannot be accounted for, or dispatch it all, and the cigar box itself, to the vault where the Academy History lies open to access by scholars. Already, I hear, the History is not infrequently consulted by persons with an interest in nineteenth- and early-twentieth-century Anglicized education. (If my reader is such a one, he should recall that for the use of citations he ought of course to ask permission of Morgan.)

I shrink from the latter course more out of caution than fear. To honor my father's memory, I am obliged to defend the family name. I foresee that to submit for preservation an eccentricity so extreme may easily provoke accusations of innate instability, not to say lunacy. At my father's graveside, I recall, my poor mother, ringed round by Wilkinsons, was made to endure the mutterings of such calumnies: hence the probability of disgrace.

It is betrayal that terrifies. Often and often in my cowardly memoir, I have been tempted to claim Ben-Zion Elefantin's voice. Logic insists on it. Reason demands it. Logic and reason are themselves cowardly. What is it I am afraid to consent to? That I am beguiled by the enigma of memory? And can memory, like dream, fabricate what ordinary consciousness cannot?

*

February 7, 1950. Of late I have been reconsidering the usefulness of having my father's artifacts appraised. What point to my keeping them here in this modernist den, where newness is king? Who will care for them as my father cared, and I after him? Who will be moved by their antiquity? For my son, who never knew his grandfather and anyhow shuns the ancestral, an inheritance of this kind can be no more than an unwanted burden. (As when the Irish maid, with her repellent brogue, recoils from what she calls my filthy pots and ugly dolls.)

Nevertheless, it may be that my father in his

Egyptian ramblings may have happened upon objects of actual consequence, worthy perhaps of some museum vitrine. My hope is that a curator's expertise may validate (dare I say it?) his life. My own craving I keep underground: only suppose that this red-kneed beaker should in fact prove to be the last remnant of Khnum on that stork-mobbed island in the middle of the Nile?

And if so?

*

February 9, 1950. The decision is made. So certain am I of its rectitude that I would engrave it in stone if I could. I will dispose of my memoir. Possibly I will quietly place it in the trash for the maid to remove. Possibly I will find a more trustworthy solution: but I will be rid of it.

A consultant from the Metropolitan Museum's History of Near Eastern Art department has agreed to view my father's artifacts. He makes no promises. So many of these amateur collections, he told me, reflect the collector's enthusiasm more than his skills or his judgment. That your father worked for a season with Sir Flinders Petrie and engaged with him privately is delightful to know, but entirely irrelevant. And that he retained notes from those conversations, even if of papyri and temples, may be of some personal interest to his son, but is hardly more generally useful. More frequently than not, what is brought to our attention is meaningless detritus, or worse, inept forgeries.

It disappointed me that despite my insistence on the authenticity of Sir Flinders Petrie's signature, he declined so much as to glance at my father's notebook. His dismissal persuades me also to destroy it. If for the expert it holds no scientific or historical value, it must carry the same peril as my memoir. And should after my demise those oddments of my Wilkinson cousins (they are included in my will) come upon either notebook or memoir, their ill-natured suspicions of my father's madness will be confirmed.

My father, then, was an enthusiast. That he anointed his Cousin William, that he was besotted with Cousin William for all of his days, was that mad?

*

February 12, 1950. Lincoln's Birthday. The question of the deposition, as I hereafter will term it, secreted in this faintly odorous antiquated box: I must finally call it a deposition, as if it were somehow rendered under oath, never mind that its authorship is ambiguous. Or if it is instead an apologia pro vita sua, then whose entrails is it exposing, whose disordered will?

I am today taken by surprise by a parcel sent to me here from Morgan Bank. John Theory writes that though the late Reverend Henry McLeod Greenhill's library had suffered constant serious deterioration due to the unfortunate location of its place of storage, in addition to the ravages of insect infestation, and could not be preserved, it seemed prudent to draw up an inventory of its holdings as a supplement to the History of the Temple Academy for Boys by Many Hands (1915), kept here in the vault containing other pertinent Academy materials for which Morgan is now responsible, including an unattributed Sargent portrait of the author Henry James, Jr. And since you, his letter continues, as the sole remaining Trustee whose present address is known, and in view of your ongoing interest in the Academy, a copy of said inventory is herewith enclosed. With kind regards, JT.

These multitudinous lists consist of scores and scores of esoteric titles, some in German and French, a cluster of Greek and Latin grammars, a threadbare copy of Gibbon's Decline and Fall of the Roman Empire, whole shelves of theological studies (Augustine, Origen, Tertullian, and so forth), a History of the Jews (translated from the German, with pencilled notes), and an abundance of volumes related to the early Levant: Development of Epigraphy; Tells of Mesopotamia, Babylon, Nimrud, and Nineveh; Yahweh and the Gods of Canaan, and on and on.

One title among the last catapults me, if I may put it so, into wild surmise. I give it below, as it appears in the inventory:

The Israelite Temple on Elephantine Island, Volume II. Reconstructive diagrams. Maps, including surrounding area. History of tripartite temples. The Khnumian cultic niche. Author: Douglas C. Hesse, Ph.D. Oriental Press, 1912. [Volume I missing.]

Volume I missing? How? Where? Into whose fancies did it go? And what is it that unnerves me so?

*

February 17, 1950. The building is being rapidly populated. When I go down for my walk, I am no longer alone in the elevator. Three or four times a week a young Japanese woman and her little son join me there. Her face is flawless porcelain, and I think of Miranda's favorite vase (the willowy maiden on the bridge) and its pride of place on that mahogany console I so much disliked. In our companionable two-minute descent I learn that her husband is second in rank at the Japanese consulate. At half-past three, when school is out, the lobby, with its hideous spider-legged Saarinen chairs (so I am told they are called), is clamorous with the squeals of a flock of children, nearly all of them accompanied by white-shoed nannies. I have yet to see here the silver heads of widows and widowers: am I the only aged occupant? My own silver head is thoroughly overlooked, my name unrecognized: all these ripe and pulsing lives making their way, climbing their rungs, bedding their beloveds, have no use for a retired Trustee of a forgotten patrician academy.

I am no one's decoy. I live here on the

strength of another boy's honest gratitude. And for what? That a Petrie never called him Hebe?

*

February 18, 1950. When I am at times too fatigued for my afternoon walk, I sit in the lobby on these comfortless chairs to watch the children come home from school. They put me in mind of birds, always flitting, always chirping, and their quick eyes dart like the eyes of birds, and their cheeks are round and their little brown shoes are buckled and their satchels are of many colors, and when they shout, as they often do, they make a tangled soprano chorus. Strange to find myself among children after years of mouldering in the company of old men. I have picked out one or two of my favorites, the small Japanese boy, always with his mother, and an older girl whose unaware breasts, as I imagine, are already budding. Now and then I catch sight of a child of perhaps eleven or twelve who seems to hold himself apart, and never romps as the others do, but hurries away, though I never see where, and before I can steal a glance at his face. What marks him for me is his blood-red hair.

★

March 12, 1950. For the last few weeks I have not been entirely myself, and while the weather is bright and I am exacting in my dress even when confined, I am never tempted to walk. I am content enough with the services offered here, despite the incompetence of the laundress who delivers my personal things: time after time, this annoyance of mismatched socks carelessly returned to their drawer where I habitually find them. Luckily, among the promised amenities is a personal shopper who replenishes my socks (without getting rid of the useless singles), and also my shirts, continually speckled with ink on the sleeves. Nor do I miss sitting alone at a restaurant table, while the tables all around are noisy with prattle and cackle. As for room service, the trays arrive on a prettified cart, and depart with not a word beyond Sir and Good Morning. Even the wretched Amelia, and surely Hedda with her Freud and her stews and her Heine, gave proof of the reality of human flesh.

So I turn again and again to the riddles in my father's cigar box. Not to pass the time, as old people do, but out of an insistence that grapples me more and more. I am hypnotized, if you will, by a certain passage in the deposition: the capsule of all. The significant thing, the significant thing. It shakes me, it unmans me. I mean to penetrate the intent of those implausible traders in search of an implausible goal. (And wasn't my father just such a trader?) Is it, the significant thing, made of clay, of stone, what form does it take, is it weighty, is it slight, is it palpable at all, like a body or a bird? Or is it a fanatical dream? Then whose?

Or is it a mighty idea?

★

May 30, 1950. Memorial Day. Since henceforth I will have no reader, I need not say by what means I have disposed of my memoir, and my father's notebook with it. Enough to know that they are, like all things treasonous, banished.

The deposition itself I have concealed where only my son is likely to find it when he comes to search among my personal effects to choose how I am to be clothed for my burial. (There will be no funeral.) Hence I can freely disclose in these final reflections the site of its unearthing: a cigar box beneath the innumerable socks accumulated in a crowded drawer.

I have not been well for many weeks. The doctor who serves this place belittles my complaints. Not illness, he asserts. Social malaise, that despicable cant. No letters come, and except for the obituaries (so many of my peers, familiar names) I have lost all concern for the newspaper's cataclysms.

I have had a single visitor. Hedda, uninvited. Surprisingly, on the advice of the defectors that there were still jobs to be had, she is now employed as one of the newer cooks at the Oyster Bar. She was eager to tell that she had lately observed a Judge Greenhill at a table with a view of the ramp, a lebhaftig and talkative old man, and can it be true that I knew him as a child at the Academy? (I did see that Ned's wife died early in April.) She brought me a pastry, charmingly wrapped. I am afraid our conversation was sparse. She wished me well and departed.

But I cannot eat something so unbearably sweet.

*

I give this writing no date. I am unsure of the date. I dislike putting on my shoes. The windows cannot be opened. There are no fans here in summer. The air conditioning blows cold.

I think I know the significant thing. Ben-Zion Elefantin too knows the significant thing.

Only the two of us know.

Not in the heavens, not in the sea, not a god

made of stone buried in the earth. A temple in a lost kingdom of storks on the Nile, is that what it is?

Only the two of us know.

We two kings.

Acknowledgments

For entry into the world of Sir Flinders Petrie, I am indebted to the archaeologists Rachel Hallote and Alexander Joffe, from whom I learned that though stories can never generate pots, pots will always tell stories.

—C.O.

A NOTE ON THE TYPE

This book was set in a version of the well-known Monotype face Bembo. This letter was cut for the celebrated Venetian printer Aldus Manutius by Francesco Griffo, and first used in Pietro Cardinal Bembo's *De Aetna* of 1495.

The companion italic is an adaptation of the chancery script type designed by the calligrapher and printer Lodovico degli Arrighi.

Composed by North Market Street Graphics, Lancaster, Pennsylvania

Printed and bound by LSC Communications, Crawfordsville, Indiana

Designed by Soonyoung Kwon